Book Express
Quality and Value in Every Book...

Specially produced for Book Express, Inc.

Airport Business Center,

29 Kripes Road,

East Granby, Connecticut, USA.

North American Direct Sales rights in this edition are

exclusive to Book Express Inc.

Rabbits In Trouble!

Ana Rosa Marti
Adapted by Judy Grosset
Illustrated by Carmelo Garmendia

Contents

Sick Tricks

Grey Ears woke up one morning to find Brown Ears standing by the side of the bed looking exceedingly grumpy.

"Good morning, Brown Ears. Why the grumpy face on such a fine day?" he asked, stretching and yawning.

"There's no dandelion tea for breakfast, and I suppose it's my turn to go and get it!" grumbled Brown Ears. "I suppose it's my turn, because it always seems to be my turn, and that's why I'm grumpy!"

"Oh don't be so silly!" scolded Grey Ears. "As a matter of fact it is your turn as I have done the shopping for the last three days in a row, but seeing as it is such a beautiful morning, I shall spare you the bother and go for the dandelion tea myself!" With that, Grey Ears cheerily hopped out of bed, put on his clothes, and marched off to the shops.

After he had gone, Brown Ears cheered up considerably. He was really quite a lazy little rabbit, and it was nice to be saved the effort of trailing to the shops. It was nice to have a friend to run after him. It was just a pity that Grey Ears didn't do what Brown Ears wanted all the time. As he was thinking this, a plan was forming in his head. His nose twitched with delight at the very thought. He could get Grey Ears to run around after him, seeing to his every need! All that it would take was a little bit of acting.

Hastily he rummaged in his bedroom cupboard until he found a great big old woolly blanket.

Then he moved his favourite armchair right next to the stove, as close as it would go, and stoked up the stove until it was roasting hot. After a little bit of posing and practising in front of the mirror, he wrapped himself in the blanket, settled himself comfortably in the armchair, and waited for Grey Ears to come back from the shops.

When Grey Ears returned a little while later, he found a very different Brown Ears to the one he had spoken to only minutes before. This Brown Ears was sitting huddled by the stove, wrapped in blankets, with a very sorry expression indeed on his face.

"What on earth is the matter with you, Brown Ears?" he asked in surprise.

"I'm ill, Grey Ears," answered his friend flatly "And I'm afraid I'm going to be ill for at least a week. I'm afraid that I shall have to rely on you to look after me – oh, and I'm sorry about the housework. Of course I would dearly love to help you out, Grey Ears, but I am afraid that I am simply far too weak. I shall probably need a diet of rich and nourishing food, in fact, to aid my recovery. Oh, how my head aches! Could you go and get my breakfast for me, Grey Ears, before I faint?"

Grey Ears meekly left the room and went into the kitchen to prepare breakfast, without a word of argument.

Brown Ears settled himself comfortably in his chair and smiled.

This was a marvellous game to play!

However, Brown Ears did not realise just how well his little friend knew him. Through in the kitchen, Grey Ears was quietly preparing breakfast for Brown Ears, but at the same time he was working out how to beat Brown Ears at his own game. He knew full well that Brown Ears was not ill at all!

Seeing Maurice Mouse passing by the window, he popped out and asked him to call round at Dr Squirrel's surgery and ask him to pay a visit to the rabbits' house. "Ill for at least a week, eh?" he said to himself. "We'll soon see about that!"

Dr Squirrel soon arrived, looking very smart indeed in the shiny top hat which he used for calling upon patients. Grey Ears met him at the door.

Now to set about his revenge! Brown Ears was really rather scared of Dr. Squirrel, and Grey Ears knew this very well. Grey Ears was going to enlist Dr Squirrel's help in making life a lot less easy for the invalid Brown Ears!

"Thank you for coming, Dr Squirrel," he said. "I don't know if you will like what I have to say to you. Brown Ears tells me that he is feeling very ill, you see, but I am afraid that I simply don't believe him. Do you think you could take a look at him for me? I could do with your assistance!"

Dr Squirrel smiled kindly at Grey Ears. He, too, knew Brown Ears and his tricks of old. "Don't worry, Grey Ears," he said. "Whether Brown Ears is truly ill or not, I think I shall be able to treat him!"

Brown Ears wasn't too happy to see Dr Squirrel at all.

"I think I am a bit too weak to be bothered with a medical examination!" he protested. "Anyone can see I'm ill, after all!"

"Quiet please, Brown Ears, and breathe in deeply!" ordered Dr Squirrel, pressing his stethoscope to Brown Ears' chest.

"I'm sure I'll have you up and about in a couple of days!" he declared when he had finished his examination.

"Oh, Doctor, I'm sure it will take longer than that!" argued Brown Ears. "I am most dreadfully ill!"

"Oh well, we will see," said Dr. Squirrel. "Now, if you will excuse me, I must discuss your treatment with your friend Grey Ears." And with that he left the room.

"Grey Ears," he said when he got out of the room, "I think a little get-Brown-Ears-to-stop-play-acting treatment is required. This is what I would like you to do"

Dr Squirrel bent down and whispered a series of instructions in Grey Ear's ear. As he whispered, he could see a smile spreading across Grey Ear's face. Grey Ears liked the sound of the doctor's plans!

When he bid goodbye to Dr Squirrel, Grey Ears was giggling in anticipation of the fun that lay ahead of him.

Meanwhile, upstairs in the bedroom, Brown Ears lay back in bed, contented, relaxed and completely unaware of the plotting between Grey Ears and Dr Squirrel down below. He was looking forward to living a life of luxury for several days!

At lunchtime Grey Ears was very busy indeed in the bedroom with Brown Ears. First, he placed a boiling hot-water bottle at his friend's feet, and a painfully cold ice-pack on his head. Then he gave him three different kinds of medicine, two large spoonfuls of each, and each one absolutely disgusting. Finally, he fed Brown Ears a large plateful of cold cucumber and nasturtium soup, which Brown Ears particularly hated.

"Grey Ears, why are you doing this to me?" he cried. "I need proper good food, like apple pies, and carrot soup, and elderberry wine! This ice-pack is killing me, and the hot-water bottle is far too hot! How can I possibly get better if I'm not looked after properly?"

"Oh Brown Ears, can't you see that I am looking after you properly? It's doctor's orders! Lots of medicine, hot feet, cold head, no rich food, and you'll be better in no time!" Grey Ears was enjoying this!

Much to Brown Ears' dismay, it was much the same at teatime. His head ached from all the ice-packs, and his feet tingled terribly from all the hot-water bottles. The medicine still tasted absolutely dreadful, and worst of all, he had to drink two platefuls of cucumber and nasturtium soup! He went to sleep that night feeling very miserable indeed. His plan didn't seem to be working at all well, and he just couldn't work out why.

Grey Ears smiled contentedly to himself as he tucked himself in for the night. One way or another, Brown Ears was going to learn his lesson!

Next morning Grey Ears hopped out of bed happily and went straight into the kitchen to prepare Brown Ears' treatment.

"No breakfast," Dr Squirrel had said. "Just medicine and ice-packs!" Grey Ears prepared the tray and went in to see Brown Ears.

"Where's my breakfast?" demanded Brown Ears.

"No breakfast today!" announced Grey Ears and repeated Dr Squirrel's orders to his friend.

At this, Brown Ears decided that he had had enough, and leapt out of bed with such force that Grey Ears got quite a fright.

"Right, that's it!" he declared. "I am going to see Dr Squirrel about this!"

Grey Ears had a little giggle to himself behind Brown Ears' back. But he did not have long to laugh, because Brown Ears was in action at once.

Angrily, he struggled into his clothes. "I'll tell that doctor just what I think of him!" he fumed. "What a way to treat a rabbit who's supposed to be sick!"

Grey Ears found it hard to conceal his amusement at all this. He knew that Dr Squirrel had found just the right way to treat Brown Ears, but he didn't dare tell that to Brown Ears!

19

"Wait for me, Brown Ears!" he called as he ran after his friend down the stairs. "Surely you shouldn't be rushing around like that in your condition!" Grey Ears could hardly keep up for trying not to laugh!

"I am going to see Dr Squirrel *right now*, and I shall give him a piece of my mind!" yelled back Brown Ears.

In no time at all, they had reached Dr Squirrel's surgery.

"Hello there, Brown Ears!" the Doctor greeted them. "It's wonderful to see you here. Didn't I tell you that I would have you up and about in no time?" He winked at Grey Ears. Brown Ears saw the wink, and all of a sudden the truth dawned on him. "Dr Squirrel! Grey Ears! You tricked me! All that horrible medicine – those freezing cold ice-packs – starving me half to death – it was all a trick!"

Dr. Squirrel had hardly time to bid farewell to the two little rabbits as Brown Ears chased Grey Ears out into the street.

"You shouldn't be running so fast in your condition, Brown Ears!" he joked as the two rabbits raced off into the distance.

Up and down the streets Brown Ears chased Grey Ears in his fury. "How could you do this to me, Grey Ears?" he yelled. "That was a dreadful trick to play on me! I thought you were my friend – wait until I catch up with you – I'll pay you back!"

"You started it, Brown Ears!" shouted back Grey Ears. "You pretended to be ill! You tried to trick me into being your slave for a week! You deserved it!"

All the time they were running they kept up the argument, but gradually as they got more and more out of breath, they yelled less and less at each other. When they finally came to a halt, completely breathless, Brown Ears' fury had abated and he could see the funny side of things.

As they puffed and panted, trying to get their breath back, the rabbits suddenly realised that they were standing outside the baker's shop.

This was a favourite place of both Grey Ears and Brown Ears. The rabbits would often stop at this window on their way through the village, and gaze in with mouths watering. The window was always jam–packed full of sticky, gooey, stodgy cakes. And so they gazed again today, their fury with each other forgotten for a moment as they took in the glorious display of goodies before their eyes.

"Don't those cakes look good?" Grey Ears asked his friend.

"Mmm – yes – that big pink sticky one looks the tastiest of all to me! And look at that lovely crusty bread!" Brown Ears remembered just how hungry he was, having had nothing to eat the day before except for medicine and cold cucumber and nasturtium soup. His tummy rumbled and his mouth began to water at the sight of all that delicious food.

It seemed a shame to carry on fighting, when it was much, much nicer to look at the food in friendly companionship. Both rabbits stood for a while in silence, wondering which one would be the first to make friends again, but not quite willing to be the only one to apologise!

Finally Grey Ears turned to his friend and said, "I'll tell you what, Brown Ears. I'll say sorry to you, if you'll say sorry to me!"

Brown Ears thought about this for a moment, "I think that's probably a good idea, Grey Ears," he agreed, "and then we can be friends again."

The two rabbits solemnly shook paws with each other and said sorry to each other most graciously.

"There's one more thing we should do to further seal our renewed friendship, Grey Ears," said Brown Ears very seriously.

"Oh, what's that?" asked Grey Ears. Brown Ears laughed.

"We should have a big sticky bun each – and *you're paying*!" he cried, dragging his friend into the baker's shop with him.

A Fair Frolic

It was the first day of the fair's visit, and Mr Hedgehog was getting ready to go along and see the fun.

He was wearing his best jacket and bow tie, and had his watch and chain on his waistcoat.

He admired himself in the mirror, checked his watch and set off for the fairground.

The fair only came to the village once a year, and it was quite an occasion for everyone.

As he walked along the High Street Mr Hedgehog thought of all the stalls, and of the prizes he might win. He had saved up all year so that he could afford to try everything.

He loved the excitement of it all – the noise, the hustle and bustle, the smell of food cooking in the open air, the brightly coloured sideshows, and the sticky feel of candy floss on his whiskers.

He felt sure he was going to have a wonderful day.

Poor Harry Hedgehog! Little did he know what lay in store for him!

And what of Grey Ears and Brown Ears?

At just about the same time, the two rabbits were also on their way to the fair from the other side of the village, but, as usual they didn't have any spending money.

"Listen," said Brown Ears to his friend. "I've got a great plan – why don't we try and earn some money at the fair?"

"Don't be silly," said Grey Ears. "You need a stall with games or something to sell; we don't have anything."

"We could try and get a job!" said Brown Ears. And when they had reached the fairground, he went off to find the fair owner.

He hunted around the stalls and tents without any success, but as he walked, his determination increased. The smell of food wafted all around him and was making him extremely hungry.

He had to make some money to buy some food.

And he had to try some of these games and rides!

He decided to ask some of the stall holders if they knew where he could find the owner.

"Excuse me," he said to the weasels at the entrance. "Have you seen the owner anywhere?"

"Look behind the big tent – you'll see him there."

Brown Ears grabbed Grey Ears and they went to find the owner together.

Brown Ears and Grey Ears were asking the owner if they could work at the fair, when Harry Hedgehog arrived, eager to begin his fun.

"One of the stalls hasn't arrived," said the owner. "Why don't you think of something to take its place?"

Brown Ears caught sight of Harry, and had an idea.

He whispered in Grey Ears' ear, "Just do everything I say, okay?" and winked.   Grey Ears nodded.

Brown Ears turned to the fair owner.   "Leave it to us, sir!" he said confidently.

Then he turned to Harry.   "If you'll just help us for five minutes, Harry, we'll let you try our sideshow for free!"

"Okay then!" Harry agreed.

Brown Ears winked at Grey Ears once more, and they set off to find their stall with the unsuspecting hedgehog in tow.

With Harry Hedgehog's help, the two rabbits found a bench, two buckets of water, and some sponges in baskets.

"What's all this for?" asked Harry.

"Oh, you'll see in a minute!" said Brown Ears. He took Grey Ears aside for a moment and whispered to him. Grey Ears giggled.

"I'll be back," said Brown Ears out loud to Grey Ears. "I've got an idea – you take Mr Hedgehog and wait for me behind the tent."

Grey Ears and Mr Hedgehog watched Brown Ears run off, and they waited behind the tent. Then it was Grey Ears' turn to disappear.

"I'll go and find a table to use for our stall – you stay here – sit down over there.," said Grey Ears pointing, to the bench.

Poor, poor Harry!   He had no idea at all that he was about to be used so cruelly.   Content with the thought that he was going to have a free shot on this mysterious sideshow in return for his help, he obediently sat down to wait on the bench as he had been told to do.

The rabbits seemed to be away for a long time, so Mr Hedgehog settled down to read a newspaper which had been lying on the bench. He had just turned to the horoscopes when *suddenly* . . . .

"*Roll up, roll up* – hit the hedgehog – win a prize!" Mr Hedgehog recognised Brown Ears' voice.

"What the . . . !!" exclaimed Mr Hedgehog.   He was being assaulted by soggy sponges!

Mr Hedgehog looked up – he couldn't believe his eyes.   Someone was throwing the sponges at him.

Constable Weasel was enjoying himself immensely, having a wonderful time.

Harry Hedgehog was not having a wonderful time, however. He was by now soaking wet from head to toe. His best jacket was positively dripping, and he could feel the water soaking right through to his underwear.

How would you feel if it had happened to you?

Mr Hedgehog was furious. He jumped up from his seat and immediately he started to throw the sponges back at Constable Weasel.

"Aah!" yelled Constable Weasel as the first sponge hit him full in the face.

"Bleh!" he spluttered as another sponge knocked his hat off, sending water cascading down the back of his neck.

"*Stop!*" he yelled, just in time to stop Harry Hedgehog from throwing another sponge at him.

Now, up until Constable Weasel shouted "*Stop*", Harry Hedgehog had been too angry to see who he had been throwing the sponges at. He had merely been throwing them in a blind rage, getting revenge for his own soaking.   All of a sudden, he realised who it was that he had been taking out his anger upon.   Poor Harry Hedgehog!   He was so embarrassed and frightened that he would be in trouble with Constable Weasel.   He turned to run away, but Constable Weasel caught him firmly by the sleeve of his jacket.   Harry Hedgehog quaked with fear at what might happen to him now, but he need not have worried.

Constable Weasel had thought that he had been throwing sponges at a dummy!   When he realised that it was Harry Hedgehog, and that Harry Hedgehog was not expecting to have sponges thrown at him, Constable Weasel had swiftly worked out what had happened.

"BROWN EARS AND GREY EARS!" he roared at the top of his voice.

Brown Ears and Grey Ears fled.

The rabbits ran for their lives, chased by Constable Weasel and a very angry Mr Hedgehog, who were armed with sponges which they were aiming at the rabbits.

"Faster," yelled Grey Ears. "They're catching up."

And so ended the rabbits' day at the fair.   They ran without stopping until they reached the safety of their own little house.   There they stayed, having earned no money and having had not a single go at any of the sideshows.

And what of the others?   After a while they gave up chasing Grey Ears and Brown Ears.   They had given the rascally pair a good fright, and that was enough.

Harry Hedgehog and Constable Weasel went home to change into dry clothes, and then they went back to join the rest of the village animals, enjoying all the fun of the fair.

Mr Badger
And The Carrots

One morning, Grey Ears woke up to find that his friend was already up and about and in a happy mood.

"Come on, wake up, sleepy head!" said Brown Ears.

"Oh?   What time is it?" asked Grey Ears sleepily.

"It's late, and time to get up."

"What's for breakfast?" yawned Grey Ears, sitting up in bed.

"What do you mean, 'What's for breakfast?'   You know there is no food in the house.   When do we ever have food in the house? – I'm starving!" complained Brown Ears.

"What are we going to do?" wailed Grey Ears.

"We'll have to find some work to earn enough money to fill the larder," said Brown Ears.

"But who's going to give us work after all the trouble we've caused?"

Brown Ears looked seriously at his friend.   "There's nothing else for it.   We'll have to turn over a new leaf.   We'll have to do a few good turns and persuade people to trust us," he said.

Grey Ears looked thoughtful.   "Mm," he said.   "I suppose it's worth a try."

The two friends got dressed and went out.   The village was bustling. Everyone was hurrying to work, except of course the two rabbits, who could only stand and watch.

"I bet they've all had breakfast," moaned Grey Ears.

The two rabbits stood for quite a while watching the world go by.

Neither of them had ever had what you would call a proper job.

They didn't know what it was like to get up early and work all day and every day.

"Why don't you get a proper job, Brown Ears?" said Grey Ears thoughtfully. "Then we would have enough money to live on without having to come up with clever schemes all the time."

"Why don't you get a job?" replied Brown Ears.

"You're much cleverer than I am. You're the one with all the ideas. You'd be much better at a proper job than I would."

The truth was that both rabbits were equally lazy and equally reluctant to try to find regular work. They had grown so used to their way of life that they would find it very difficult to change.

They spent every day wondering where their next meal was coming from, and the whole village knew it, and everyone was very, very wary of the two rabbits, who were becoming really quite unpopular with their wily ways.

Nobody would lend them anything, because they knew that they would be highly unlikely to get it back.

Nobody would trust them, for at some time or another practically everybody in the village had suffered some form of misfortune at the hands of the rascally pair.

And even when, as so often happened, the two rabbits were penniless and hungry, the other animals were unwilling to help, as they felt that Grey Ears' and Brown Ears' predicament was their own fault.

Just then, Mr Badger went past carrying a sack. A very heavy sack by the look of it, because he was walking very slowly, bent under the weight of his load.

"I know!" whispered Grey Ears softly. "We could offer to carry Mr Badger's load!"

"What a good idea," agreed Brown Ears. "Quick! I know a short cut. We'll get ahead of him. Then we can catch him when he's really tired and willing to let us help."

The rabbits set off.   Their plan was to meet Mr Badger further up the road.   They were sure that he hadn't noticed them standing watching him earlier.   They ran as fast as they could, remembering all the tricks they had played on Mr Badger in the past.

"I hope he doesn't hold any grudges against us," panted Grey Ears as they ran.

"We'll soon find out," puffed Brown Ears breathlessly.

They rounded the next corner, jumped over a fence and ran to the edge of the road that Mr Badger would be coming along very soon.

Brown Ears had been thinking to himself as they ran that he did not relish the thought of carrying that heavy sack, and as they reached the road and sat by a tree waiting for Mr Badger, he said to Grey Ears, "I think it would be best if you helped Mr Badger today.   After all, he has only one sack to carry.   There's no point in both of us offering to carry one sack is there?"

Grey Ears nodded.   "It won't take long," he said, "You stay here and wait for me, then we can go and tell everyone how helpful we've been."

"All right," said Brown Ears, smiling to himself.

"Careful – here comes Badger now!"

Brown Ears, of course, was willing to trick even his best friend into doing all the hard work for him, but Grey Ears, as usual, had been completely taken in.

Poor Grey Ears!

"Good morning, Mr Badger," said Grey Ears politely. "That looks like a heavy load you're carrying. Can I help you?"

"Well er – good morning, Grey Ears," said a rather surprised Mr Badger. "I would very much like some help, but I'll walk with you as you carry my sack to my house. I don't trust you to deliver it."

"Really, Mr Badger! You mustn't believe all the stories you hear about us. We're really very trustworthy rabbits – aren't we, Brown Ears?" exclaimed Grey Ears as he swung the heavy sack on his shoulders, and set off with Mr Badger.

"See you later!" Brown Ears called as they strode off down the path towards Badger Cottage.

Unknown to Mr Badger and Grey Ears, as the rabbit had lifted the sack from the ground, a carrot had fallen out from a hole in the bottom of it. Brown Ears had spotted it straight away.

Brown Ears waited until Grey Ears and Badger were out of sight. He stared after them and couldn't believe his eyes. There was a trail of carrots all the way down the road!

He went to fetch another sack, which he had spotted at the edge of the field, and hurried back to collect the carrots that had dropped out of the sack, and soon he had a full load.

He did not stop to think that as Grey Ears' load was getting lighter, his own was getting heavier!

He did not even realise that he was actually working; he was too busy thinking of steaming bowls of carrot soup!

Meanwhile, Grey Ears and Mr Badger had nearly reached Badger Cottage when Mr Badger noticed that the sack was nearly empty.

"So this is how you help me!" he roared, picking Grey Ears up by his collar and shaking him hard until his teeth rattled.

"You and your accomplice have plotted together to steal my crop of carrots!"

"I don't know what you mean," shrieked Grey Ears. "Honestly, I've just been trying to help!"

Mr Badger gave up. He was extremely angry. He just couldn't believe that he'd lost so much of his crop of carrots.

It was obvious that Mr Badger wasn't prepared to listen to anything that Grey Ears had to say, so the rabbit saw his chance and ran off just as fast as his frightened legs would carry him.

He had to find Brown Ears and warn him that their plan had failed.

He looked over his shoulder to see if Badger was chasing him, but Mr Badger was just standing there, shaking his fist in fury.

Brown Ears had been having a rest while he waited for his friend. He had hidden the carrots, which he had piled up behind the tree, in case anyone should come along and ask awkward questions.

He was surprised to see Grey Ears back so quickly, as it was really quite a long way to Badger's cottage.

"Quick – hide!" shouted Grey Ears. "It's all gone wrong!"

"What's happened?" asked Brown Ears.

"Badger thinks that you and I plotted to steal his carrots and doesn't believe we were just trying to help!"

"Oh, that's just terrible," said Brown Ears, smiling.

"What's so funny?" said a very puzzled looking Grey Ears. "Now we can't hope to persuade people to give us work so that we can buy food. This is a desperate situation!"

"Is it really?" said Brown Ears. "I don't think we'll be hungry for long!"

He pulled out his sack of carrots and showed it to his astonished friend.

"But – but – how did you get these?" stammered Grey Ears.

"Oh, let's just say that they fell at my feet!" grinned Brown Ears. "Now, come on, let's get home and do some cooking!"

So saying, our cheeky friend took Grey Ears by the arm, swung the sack over his shoulder, and they headed off to savour their ill-gotten gains.

Conversation Piece

The last person in the village who had spoken to Brown Ears was Constable Weasel, and that had been four whole days ago. Brown Ears was in a great deal of trouble.

"Go home, Brown Ears," Constable Weasel had said, "before I am forced to lock you in jail. And don't set foot in the High Street again until you are prepared to apologise for your behaviour. There is hardly an animal left in this village who is still prepared to speak to you. If it weren't for Grey Ears, you wouldn't have any friends left!"

Brown Ears had huffily got up and trudged off home with Grey Ears trailing along behind him.

For two days Brown Ears had stayed at home, seeing nobody but his friend, and sending Grey Ears out to the shops for him whenever he felt hungry. For two days he had quite enjoyed himself, in fact. He had plenty of peace and quiet, no boring shopping to do, and lots of time to laze about in the garden in the sunshine.

On the third day, however, the rain had come down in torrents. Brown Ears had been forced to stay inside. Without the garden and the sunshine to enjoy, Brown Ears was rather at a loss. He would not, of course, consider doing any housework – he was far too lazy to even think of that! Grey Ears was quite content to sit in a comfortable armchair and read a book, but even that was too much like work for Brown Ears. Brown Ears was *bored*.

Ask any grown-up, and they will tell you that when children are bored it often means trouble, for bored children often get up to mischief.

Brown Ears was just like a child in many ways – a bored Brown Ears often meant a naughty Brown Ears. Grey Ears knew this and was feeling rather anxious!

Brown Ears paced up and down the living room, his nose twitching with impatience. Then he went over to the window and looked gloomily out.

"I think I'll just put on my coat and splash along to the shops," he said to Grey Ears as he watched the rain dripping and splashing onto the window sill outside. "Just to see if anything is happening, you know!" he added.

"Oh no you don't, Brown Ears!" warned his friend.

"What do you mean?" asked Brown Ears.

"Have you forgotten already?" Grey Ears was surprised. "Constable Weasel has banned you from the High Street until you have apologised for all the mischief you have been causing lately! You can't just forget about what he said and go out! If he sees you when you're out he'll put you in jail for sure!"

"Oh yes, right enough, Grey Ears," said Brown Ears gloomily. "I had almost forgotten about all that. Honestly, what a fuss everybody makes about a jolly creature like me having a harmless bit of fun! You know, Grey Ears, I don't think anybody around here has much of a sense of humour at all!"

Grey Ears looked a little doubtful. He knew just how out of hand Brown Ears' "harmless fun" had become recently.

Brown Ears paced up and down the room restlessly.

Grey Ears watched him, annoyed that he couldn't concentrate on the book that he was trying to read.

Finally Brown Ears stopped pacing, stamped his foot rather crossly, and with a heavy sigh announced:

"So they want an apology, do they? All right then, they'll get one!"

For the rest of the day and almost all evening Brown Ears was busy trying to compose his apology. He found this a particularly hard thing to do because, in fact, he wasn't particularly sorry for what he had done!

Finally, after a short break and something to eat, he settled down for one last try.   He pretended that there was a monster behind him, waiting to swallow him in one gulp if he didn't finish quickly.

His imagination was so good that he made himself really scared and finished writing in three minutes flat!

Then, exhausted, he went to bed.

Next day, bright and early, Brown Ears got up and dressed himself and marched into the village, carrying a hammer, a large nail, and a piece of paper.

On the paper he had written in his best writing (which still wasn't very tidy!):

"I, Brown Ears Rabbit, do apologise
most sincerely for all the trouble that
I seem to have caused to the good
citizens of Whiskerton.   I truly did
not mean to be such a nuisance,
nor to make anybody unhappy.
I will try my best to mend my ways
and live the life of a quiet, honest
citizen in the future."

He walked over to the large oak tree in the middle of the High Street and nailed up the piece of paper for all to see.

The other animals in the street all gathered round to have a look.

"Huh! Bet he doesn't mean a word of it!" muttered Mr Mouse to Freddie Fox.

"Lot of rubbish if you ask me!" Toby Turtle remarked to no one in particular.

Without another word, every one of them turned away!

Brown Ears realised that he might be allowed in the High Street now, but in spite of his apology it seemed that the other animals were still not speaking to him.

Something would have to be done.

He set off home, and on his way he met Grey Ears, who had come along to see how his friend had got on with the other villagers.   Brown Ears told him what had happened.   "But not to worry, Grey Ears!   I have a plan!"

Grey Ears looked worried for a moment, but Brown Ears was quick to reassure him.

"Don't worry, Grey Ears, I'm not going to do anything dishonest! I'm not going to get us into any trouble!   I am simply going to take up a little hobby to pass the time.   Now, my dear fellow, would you do me a favour and get a few things from the shops for me?"

Later that morning Harry Hedgehog and Mrs Mouse stopped Grey Ears in the street.

Grey Ears was carrying an easel, some brushes and a canvas.

"What are these for?" Harry asked.

"Brown Ears," said Grey Ears with a twinkle in his eye, "has taken up painting."   And off he went home.

Back home, Grey Ears helped his wily chum to set up all his equipment.

"Don't forget to use your artist's palette to mix all your colours properly," he reminded him.

"Don't you worry, Grey Ears, I'll be mixing away like an expert in no time!" his friend beamed. "I think I might even be quite good at this!"

"That may well be true," agreed Grey Ears, "but how is it going to make the other animals start speaking to you again?"

Brown Ears took a deep breath, and adjusted the canvas on his easel.

"All I can say, Grey Ears, is that you will have to wait and see for yourself!"

For the next day and a half Brown Ears spent most of his time outside in the garden, working away at his painting.

He worked very slowly and carefully, spending a long time mixing each colour and painting tiny lines, shapes and patterns on the canvas.

"It's going to take you ages to finish at this rate!" commented Grey Ears. "What is it anyway, Brown Ears?"

"Well, what do you think it is?" said Brown Ears mysteriously.

"I'm sure I don't know!" replied his friend, puzzled. "And I still don't see how you intend to get yourself back in favour with the other villagers!"

"Wait and see, my friend, wait and see," said Brown Ears confidently.

He took a little blob of red paint and drew a tiny squiggle up in the right hand corner of the canvas. Then he stood back for a moment to admire his work.

After some consideration, he put a little green dot beside the red squiggle. Grey Ears watched him with amazement. It was a long time since he had seen his friend concentrating quite so hard as this on anything. The painting was proving to be an absorbing pastime for Brown Ears indeed!

The reason behind it all was still a bit of a mystery to Grey Ears, but he had to admit it was nice to see his friend so happy at his work!

That afternoon, Brown Ears' Uncle Ronald called round. He had heard that Brown Ears had taken up painting and was curious to see how he was getting on. He was so pleasantly surprised to see Brown Ears working so hard that he completely forgot that he wasn't speaking to him.

"I say, Brown Ears!" he exclaimed. "That's a rather nice picture! What is it exactly?"

"What do you think it is?" was all that Brown Ears would say in reply. Grey Ears was now beginning to see exactly what Brown Ears was up to!

Next morning dawned bright and sunny, and Brown Ears set up his easel in the garden once more, and carried on with his painting. Mrs Duck from the Post Office appeared behind him, peering with great interest at his work. Harry Hedgehog had indeed been spreading the news about Brown Ears' new hobby!

Just as Uncle Ronald had done, Mrs Duck opened her beak to speak to Brown Ears before she realised what she was doing.

"Oh my, Brown Ears!" she quacked. "What wonderful colours you are using in that picture. It makes me feel happy just looking at it!"

"Why, thank you, Mrs Duck," replied Brown Ears modestly.

"What are you going to call it? Is it supposed to be something, or is it an abstract?"

"Oh Mrs Duck, I'm afraid I must leave you wondering for the moment," said Brown Ears with a knowing wink, "but perhaps you will be able to understand the picture better when it's finished."

"Yes, yes, perhaps I will," agreed Mrs Duck, "but whatever it is, Brown Ears, I have to say that I think it's very pretty indeed!"

And off she waddled, having completely forgotten that Brown Ears was supposed to be out of favour.

If Harry Hedgehog had done well spreading the news about Brown Ears and his artwork, then Mrs Duck did twice as well. Mrs Duck owned the Post Office in Whiskerton. It was one of the busiest places in the village, and every animal who came in to do some business at the Post Office that day was told about Brown Ears' painting. "You mean you spoke to Brown Ears?" someone asked. "I thought that we were not going to speak to him until we were sure that he was going to change his ways!"

Mrs Duck was quick to defend herself. "Oh, I'm sure he has been behaving himself. He has been working so hard on that picture that he hasn't had time to get up to any mischief. And it's such a pretty picture – oh I wish I knew what it was supposed to be!"

Everybody now became curious to see Brown Ears' work for themselves. All anger with him seemed to be forgotten as the villagers vied with each other to guess what the picture was, or at least what it was meant to be. And, as it turned out, most of the animals liked the painting! From then on Brown Ears had a constant stream of visitors to the garden "studio".

Constable Weasel came along with Mrs Squirrel and Mrs Mole that afternoon.   He was surprisingly impressed with what he saw.   "Very nice, Brown Ears, very nice indeed!" he found himself saying.

"Why, thank you, Constable Weasel! That's just about the nicest thing you've ever said to me!" exclaimed Brown Ears.

"Can't begin to think what you might call it though," admitted Constable Weasel.

"You'll find out sooner or later!" beamed Brown Ears.

Sammy Squirrel and Mrs Mouse were the next to call upon the artist. Mrs Mouse had plenty of ideas about what the painting was supposed to be, but Brown Ears firmly told her that she was completely wrong. Poor Mrs Mouse!   She was really quite cross.   She hated secrets, and this secret was one which particularly irritated her!

Sammy Squirrel said very little, but looked at the picture very admiringly indeed.

This particularly pleased Brown Ears for Sammy Squirrel, just like his uncle, Dr Squirrel, was a very clever animal with good taste.

For him to like Brown Ears' painting was quite a compliment!

And so it went on all afternoon, and all the next day; visitor after visitor called at the rabbits' house. Grey Ears was amazed at how well Brown Ears' plan had worked. Brown Ears had been very clever indeed. All the villagers had put all thought of Brown Ears' previous bad behaviour completely out of their heads. Only two days ago they would have avoided speaking to him at all costs – today they were crowding in to see him and talk to him.

Brown Ears had realised that curiosity is a powerful thing!

The mystery of the painting, and what it was meant to be, had aroused everybody's curiosity. Everybody wanted to know the answer, and a lot of the animals thought they might have it. "Is it a tree in blossom?" asked one.

"Don't be silly! It has no trunk!" said another.

"Is it a picture of a dream that you have had?" asked somebody else.

Brown Ears gave nothing away, but kept on painting, slowly and carefully, a dab here, a splash there, all the time smiling secretly to himself.

The arguments among the onlookers went on around him as his painting slowly progressed. Brown Ears was very careful not to paint too fast, however, because he didn't want to finish while the visitors were still there. You see not even Brown Ears knew what he was painting – he had only started the picture to get people to talk to him again. He hadn't thought of a title for it at all!

Late that evening, when the last of the visitors had gone, Brown Ears put the finishing touches to his painting and sat down in a chair to survey his handiwork. He was rather proud of his efforts; it was a nice painting, full of rich colour and intricate pattern. "I wonder what I will call it?" he thought idly to himself. But all the fresh air and all the work and all the visitors had taken their toll. He was too tired to think. He was too tired to move! He fell asleep right where he was, in the chair in the garden.

"Luckily it didn't rain during the night!" Brown Ears was woken next morning by the voice of Harry Hedgehog. "It would have ruined your lovely painting! Sorry if I disturbed you, but I just wanted to ask you if you would be willing to sell it to me! I know just the spot where I could hang that picture in my house!"

Brown Ears was delighted. He had never dreamt that anyone would want to buy his picture!

Harry toddled off to get some vegetables and money to pay for it.

"This has worked out even better than I could have imagined!"
Brown Ears told Grey Ears when Harry had gone.   "I haven't been in
trouble for days, everybody is friends with me again, and I am going to
earn some money!"

Grey Ears was delighted for his friend.

"Don't forget to sign the painting like a true artist!" he reminded him.

"Righto!" said Brown Ears and signed with a flourish.

A Little while later, a very pleased Harry Hedgehog came to take possession of his new picture.   In return he gave Brown Ears half a dozen beautiful cabbages, some carrots and five pound coins.

"By the way, Brown Ears, what is the painting called?" he asked before he set off for home.

"After some thought, Harry, I have decided not to give it a name as such.   Let's just say it's a conversation piece!" said Brown Ears, laughter in his eyes.

Brown Ears was back in favour with the villagers – but for how long, I wonder?

And what of his painting? Well, he did do more paintings from time to time when he needed some peace and quiet, or when he found himself at a loose end. Some were good enough to sell, some he gave away as presents, but none quite managed to match up to his first, great Conversation Piece!

Missing

One morning Grey Ears decided to take a walk through the forest to the next village to see his grandmother.

"Make sure she gives you something nice to bring home for supper!" joked Brown Ears.

"That's not funny, Brown Ears!" scolded his friend. "You know that my grandmother is very poor. It would be quite wrong to take food from her!"

"I'm sorry, Grey Ears," said Brown Ears. "I didn't really mean it."

A little while later, Brown Ears waved his friend goodbye at the front door.   Grey Ears was looking very smart indeed, wearing his very best clothes, all neatly pressed, and his Sunday hat was ready to be perched neatly between two well-scrubbed ears.

"Goodbye, Brown Ears!" he called cheerily as he set off down the street.   "I should be back quite soon after lunch.   Grandmother gets tired easily so I don't want to stay too long with her."

Off he set through the village, feeling rather proud of himself in his smart outfit. Everybody he passed noticed that he was looking unusually neat and tidy. "Why, Grey Ears!" they exclaimed. "We can hardly recognise you! What are you and Brown Ears up to this time?"

"Nothing!" retorted Grey Ears. "I'm going to visit my grandmother in the village beyond the forest, and I want her to see me looking my very best!"

But Constable Weasel was suspicious of Grey Ears. He followed him quite a long way along the road, writing things in his notebook and asking questions in a loud cross voice. "I don't trust you and your friend, Grey Ears! Where are you going? Why are you going there? How do I know whether you are telling me the truth?" Grey Ears thought he would never be able to get away, but at the edge of the forest Constable Weasel finally gave up to let him carry on by himself.

It was quite a long walk through the forest for Grey Ears, but it was a lovely day and he enjoyed listening to the birdsong in the trees above his head, and smelling the sweet scent of the honeysuckle and wild roses which were dotted here and there among the many shrubs and bushes along the way.   All the same, he was a little nervous at the thought of his return journey.   His grandmother did so like to chat, and if she kept him talking too long, then Grey Ears would have to walk back home in the dark.   The forest was quite spooky at night, so Grey Ears hoped he would get away from his grandmother in time to avoid going through it in the darkness.

Back in the village, Brown Ears spent a very quiet morning.   After a delicious lunch of carrot stew, he sat down in his favourite armchair and closed his eyes for a little rest – just long enough to let his lunch settle properly in his tummy, he thought to himself.   He didn't have a little rest – he had a very big rest! In fact, he fell fast asleep in that armchair and snored his furry little head off until it was nearly time for tea.

He woke up, feeling a rumbling in his tummy that told him it was time for some food, and he looked around for Grey Ears.   There was no sign of him.

"He should be back home by now," thought Brown Ears, and he set off to see if Grey Ears had stopped somewhere in the village on his way home.   He wanted to know why his friend was late.

Outside in the street Brown Ears asked all the villagers he met whether they had seen Grey Ears that afternoon.   They had all seen Grey Ears in the morning, resplendent in his best clothes on his way to his grandmother's, but not one of them had seen him coming back. Brown Ears began to get a little worried.

"Perhaps he's popped in to see Mrs Mole on his way home." Brown Ears thought to himself. Brown Ears and Grey Ears often called into Mrs Mole's for a visit. She was renowned in Whiskerton for her wonderful cooking, and the two rabbits were always hoping for a taste of whatever dish she was preparing. There was just a chance that, finding himself hungry after his journey, Grey Ears had called at Mrs Mole's in the hope that there might be a spare tasty morsel for him to nibble.

However, when Brown Ears got to Mrs Mole's house he was disappointed. There was no sign of Grey Ears. Brown Ears then tried Mrs Squirrel's sweet shop and Harry Hedgehog's allotment, where Grey Ears often went when he was hungry, but with no luck.

This was a real problem. Grey Ears was never late home. Like Brown Ears, he was always hungry and would not want to miss his tea or his supper. It was getting late now, and soon it would be dark. There was only one answer: something terrible must have happened to Grey Ears. Brown Ears must get help immediately.

"I think Grey Ears may be lost – perhaps even kidnapped!" he exclaimed to the villagers. "I need some people to help me come and look for him. Can any of you come?"

"Ha, ha, Brown Ears!" they retorted. "You've tried tricks like this before! Don't think you can fool us so easily this time! Go and play your joke on somebody else!"

It was the same everywhere that Brown Ears went.   Nobody
believed him. Some people just laughed at him; others became very
angry indeed; and Mrs Duck even slammed the door of her house in
his face.

Poor Brown Ears. He sat down on the pavement and cried. It seemed that after all his tricks and nonsense nobody thought it possible that this time he could be telling the truth. And poor Grey Ears! Lost out there with nobody to find him. Brown Ears would just have to search for his friend all by himself.

He dried his eyes, dusted himself down, and set off in a determined fashion towards the forest. It was getting dark now, and he was feeling a little bit nervous about going into the forest alone, so to keep up his courage he muttered to himself as he went along: "I must find poor Grey Ears. I must find poor Grey Ears." He walked right past Constable Weasel without even noticing him. Constable Weasel saw the tear stains on Brown Ears' face.

"I wonder what's wrong with that rascal?" he said to himself, as he walked on. He came upon a group of villagers and asked them what was the matter with Brown Ears. "Oh, he's trying to pretend that Grey Ears is lost or kidnapped," they scoffed. "Of course, we don't believe him."

"I'm not so sure that he's pretending this time," said Constable Weasel. "It is my duty as a police constable to protect the animals of this village. If this is a joke then of course the rabbits will be in serious trouble. But although it may seem like a nuisance I must go and look for Grey Ears. And I must have some other animals to help me search. The forest is very big, and it is getting darker and darker. Go and get some more animals to help, all of you ! We must set off at once !"

Constable Weasel's words alarmed the villagers. After all, it was certainly true that no one had seen Grey Ears since that morning, and Brown Ears was perhaps genuinely upset.

The two rabbits could be a great nuisance, that was true, but nobody would wish them to come to any harm.

Rosie Rabbit became quite distressed. "Oh, poor Grey Ears!" she wailed.

Mrs Mouse was likewise overcome, and Rosie and she cried bitterly as the other villagers spread the news of the search.

After a few minutes, a large group of villagers had gathered together. They hurried along the road towards the forest, led by Constable Weasel. Everybody was very worried by now. "Don't worry, I'm sure we'll find Grey Ears soon," he said to comfort them. But by now it was very dark, and even he was a little bit scared.

Suddenly, they heard a funny noise. Everyone stopped. They
listened again. A sort of "shuffle" then a quiet "boohoo", and then a
rustling! Carefully, they peered over the top of the bushes. What
could it be! What a relief! It was only Brown Ears, crying his eyes out,
poor rabbit. "Don't cry, Brown Ears, we've come to help you!" they
told him, and took him along with them.

They searched behind trees, under bushes, and in every place they
could think of. No sign of Grey Ears. They searched until they were
nearly too tired to go on searching.

And then, at last, they heard another noise, coming from some
bushes.

Constable Weasel shone his torch on the bushes.   There was a pair
of very familiar grey ears sticking out !

"Grey Ears!" cried Brown Ears, pulling his friend out of the bushes,
and giving him a great big hug.   "What happened to you?

I've been so worried!"

Grey Ears looked very ashamed of himself.   He began his explanation:

"I was very nearly home, Brown Ears, when I remembered my hat!"

"Your hat?" interrupted Brown Ears.

"Yes, my hat, Brown Ears. I left it at my grandmother's" house! I was going back to get it, but I wasn't really thinking where I was supposed to be going. I took a wrong turning, and I got lost! Then it got dark, and I got scared, so I just hid in the bushes; I am so glad that you found me!"

The happy band then made their way back to the village.

Next day, after a good night's sleep to recover from their adventure, the two rabbits were out for a stroll.

"You know, Grey Ears," said Brown Ears, "you shouldn't be scared of the dark in the forest. I certainly wasn't!"

Grey Ears believed him.

Do you?

Good Intentions

"What are you reading, Grey Ears?" Brown Ears asked his little friend one evening. Grey Ears had his nose buried deep in a very big and important-looking book.

"This is very interesting, you know," said Grey Ears. "It's a book about old traditions, and this bit is all about New Year's resolutions. They seem like a good idea to me!"

"What are New Year's resolutions then, Grey Ears? Are they a good way to make money or something?" Brown Ears was interested.

His friend shook his head.

"No, no, Brown Ears, nothing like that. Let me explain. At the end of every year, on New Year's Eve, you sit down and make a list of all the things that you have been doing wrong that you want to change."

"Like what?" asked Brown Ears.

"Well, perhaps you are very untidy, or perhaps you eat too many sweet things, or tell lies or have been unkind to somebody. . . ."

"Stop! I see what you mean!" squeaked Brown Ears. He was getting embarrassed by this list of wrongdoing, for he knew well that he was guilty of all these things! Grey Ears looked at Brown Ears very sternly for a moment then continued: "Well, you make a list of all the things, and then you make another list, promising not to do them in the New Year. These promises are New Year's resolutions. Once New Year has come, you try your very best to turn over a new leaf and to keep the resolutions."

"It all sounds a bit like hard work. . ." said Brown Ears thoughtfully.

"Yes," agreed Grey Ears, "but it shows people that you are trying to improve and change your ways. Don't you think it would be nice, Brown Ears, if people really believed that we were making an effort to change our ways and behave ourselves? Just think of all the people in the village who hardly speak to us because of all the things we've done to them in the past; wouldn't it be wonderful if they became our friends again? It's just a pity that it isn't New Year just now, for I can tell you, Brown Ears, some New Year's resolutions might just do us some good!"

Brown Ears nodded thoughtfully, and both rabbits were silent for a moment. Then Brown Ears jumped up excitedly.

"Why wait for New Year? It's Midsummer's Eve tomorrow, isn't it? Let's make some Midsummer's resolutions! Nobody will care that it isn't New Year. They'll just be pleased to hear that we two have turned over a new leaf and are trying to behave for a change! First thing tomorrow, Grey Ears, we'll make our list. Then we'll give out copies all around the village so that everybody knows what good rabbits we're going to be. We'll make friends with everybody again, and everything will be wonderful!"

Grey Ears looked at his friend in delight. Just for once, it looked as if Brown Ears had thought of a plan that wouldn't get them into trouble. It was almost too good to be true!

103

That night the rabbits slept the sleep of the just, dreaming of the future that awaited them as newly upright and honest citizens of Whiskerton, respected by all the other animals. "Honesty is the best policy," as Grey Ears' Uncle Ronald always used to say, and that night at least, Brown Ears was determined to make the very best effort to follow his Uncle's good advice.

The two rabbits were up at the crack of dawn the next day, making up their list of resolutions.

"Golly, this is hard work, Grey Ears!" said Brown Ears. "I hadn't really thought about it before, but we've done so many things wrong that it takes an awfully long time to write about them all!"

Grey Ears could only agree. The list seemed endless; if they didn't make it shorter in some way, they would never be finished before the end of the day.

In the end they decided to write down only the things that they did most often and resolve not to do them again, and then at the end of

their list of resolutions they wrote: "We both know we are guilty of many other wrongdoings and hereby promise to do our very best not to do any of them again either."   Having done that, the two rabbits had completed their list by lunchtime, and had also written out several other copies to stick up around the village for all to see.   After a welcome bowl of carrot soup and some lovely crusty bread, they set off to deliver the copies to prominent places in the village.

By mid-afternoon the village was buzzing with excitement. "Just look, Mrs Mole!" exclaimed Mrs Duck at the Post Office, pointing to the list of resolutions newly pinned to her wall in a smart wooden frame. "They've promised never to play with my rubber date stamps again, or to break my parcel weighing scales. Remember how Brown Ears used to sit on them to weigh himself? He's so heavy they broke every time! These resolutions are wonderful news! Now, Mrs Mole, would you please look after the shop for me for a little while? I promised Grey Ears that I would take one of these lists over to Dr Squirrel's house for him!"

Mrs Mole took up position behind the Post Office counter instead of Mrs Duck, and Mrs Duck slipped off upstairs to get ready to go. She was pleased to see Grey Ears and Brown Ears were ready to mend their ways, and she wanted to do something to encourage them.

As she looked in the mirror to check that her new hat was on straight, Mrs Duck had an idea. On her way back from Dr Squirrel's she would deliver a nice apple pie to Grey Ears' and Brown Ears' house. These good intentions deserved to be rewarded, and a tasty pie would make a lovely reward!

Harry Hedgehog, meanwhile, could not believe what he was reading!
He had been given a copy of the rabbits' resolutions to put up outside
the village allotments, and there, fourth item on the list, was written:

"We promise to stop stealing carrots and lettuces or anything else that grows in Harry Hedgehog's allotment."

This was marvellous news – simply marvellous news!

"I think I'll give the rabbits a pound or two of carrots as a gesture of appreciation," he thought to himself. "I know that Brown Ears finds my vegetables particularly tasty."

Outside the Police Station another copy had been pinned to the door, and a crowd had gathered round to read it. "Look here, Constable Weasel, it says that Grey Ears and Brown Ears are going to stop giving you so much extra work to do!" said Percy Pig.

"Well, that's certainly good news if it's true!" replied Constable Weasel. "Life will be much easier for me in the future if these rascals really do mean to behave themselves!" He was so pleased that he rushed home to tell his wife, who made some poppy seed cake for the rabbits immediately as a reward.

And so it went on throughout the afternoon.   By teatime the rabbits had quite a selection of goodies in their store cupboard, given by the village people in gratitude for them turning over a new leaf.

"It's lucky for us you read that book last night, Grey Ears!" exclaimed Brown Ears. "Who gave the book to you?"

"Oh, Rosie Rabbit lent it to me," answered Grey Ears. "Perhaps we should do something to say thank you to her!"

"Perhaps we should indeed," agreed Brown Ears. "Hold on right there!" He dashed out of the door.

While Brown Ears was away, Grey Ears busied himself with putting away all the food that they had been given.   By the time he had finished, the pantry and store cupboard were both full to bursting.

Shortly afterwards Brown Ears returned, armed with a beautiful, big bunch of flowers.   "Let's take these over to Rosie Rabbit as a thank you present," he suggested. "We've just got time before tea."

"Good idea!" said Grey Ears, and the two rabbits set off.

Rosie Rabbit was very impressed with the flowers. "These are quite beautiful, my dears!" she exclaimed. "It was lovely to hear such good news about you two today, I must say! Come in and have your tea with me before you go back home. I'm making mushroom surprise and apple turnover!"

The two rabbits did not hesitate. The very thought of such a delicious meal made their mouths water, and the food they had at home would keep.

Much later, after a lovely evening at Rosie's, the two rabbits were back home and preparing for sleep.   They had eaten a great deal at Rosie's but had still found room for a small snack before they settled down for the night.

"What a super day we've had!" cried Brown Ears. "We've got enough food to keep us going for weeks.   I wish we'd thought of this before!" Crumbs from Mrs Duck's apple pie flew from his lips as he spoke.

"It has been good, hasn't it, Brown Ears?" sighed Grey Ears contentedly.   "But we must try hard now to keep those resolutions that we made.   They were promises after all!"

Brown Ears put his plate aside and was just about to snuggle down

under the sheets when Grey Ears suddenly had a thought.

"By the way, Brown Ears, where did you get those flowers?"

"What flowers?" asked Brown Ears.

"You know perfectly well what flowers!" said Grey Ears, frowning.

"Oh, yes, those flowers!" said Brown Ears, slowly sitting up in bed. "Well," he said, grinning gleefully "I went down to the allotments, and while Harry Hedgehog was busy showing Deirdre Dormouse the list of our resolutions, I just slipped behind his back and picked a few of his choicest blooms!"

"*Brown Ears*!" exclaimed Grey Ears. "I despair of you! Is there no chance of your changing your ways?"

What do you think?

Burning Ambitions

Old Sam Squirrel's sweet shop was a delight. It sold everything sweet and sticky that you could possibly imagine. Grey Ears loved to go in just to look around and see all the goodies and dream about what he would buy if he had the money. One cold autumn morning he was doing just that, when Sam Squirel asked him, "Why do you come in here so often when you hardly ever buy anything?"

Startled out of his daydream, Grey Ears gave a little jump.

"Oh–um–I just like to look, that's all. I can't really afford to buy anything at the moment. In fact, I can't often afford to buy anything, Brown Ears and I hardly ever seem to have any money, but this time I can't afford to buy anything because we're trying to save up to buy fireworks. It'll soon be Guy Fawkes Night, and we want a really good display." Grey Ears looked a little wistful - "These humbugs do look good though!"

It was Grey Ears'' lucky day. Sam Squirrel was in a good mood.

"I'll tell you what, Grey Ears," he said, "I have to go out on business for a little while tomorrow afternoon. I was going to shut up the shop, but perhaps you and your friend can help me out. If you both mind the shop for me while I am away, I shall pay you with a bag of humbugs and a box of fireworks."

Grey Ears was beside himself with joy. Humbugs and fireworks? It was a dream come true!

"I'll be back after lunch tomorrow!" he squeaked, and rushed off to find Brown Ears.

Brown Ears, too, was delighted when he heard the news that night. But one box of fireworks didn't seem like quite enough for the really wonderful display that he had in mind.

"We still need some more money, Grey Ears. And if we're working all afternoon in Sam's shop we can't earn any money anywhere else, and it's Guy Fawkes Night tomorrow night! We need a plan!"

Grey Ears looked concerned. Brown Ears thought hard for a moment and then beamed.

"I have the very idea, Grey Ears! A penny for the Guy! That's what people do, after all, isn't it? They make a dummy to burn on the bonfire, a model of Guy Fawkes, and before the bonfire they show it to people to earn money to buy fireworks. We must do just that! We'll take a Guy to Sam's shop tomorrow, and it can earn money for us

while we are working."

"But we haven't time to make a good Guy!" protested Grey Ears. "These things are difficult to make!"

"You have a point there," agreed Brown Ears, "but what if I was to tell you that we didn't need to make a Guy?"

"What do you mean?" asked Grey Ears suspiciously.

"Wait until morning, and I'll show you !" exclaimed his friend.

Grey Ears didn't really want to wait until morning to find out what his friend had in mind, but he didn't have much choice in the matter. Within a couple of minutes, Brown Ears was under the covers and fast asleep.

Next morning, Brown Ears had some hard work persuading Grey

Ears to go along with his plan, but by lunchtime he had talked him into it.   Grey Ears was to be the Guy! As soon as old Sam Squirrel had left the shop, Brown Ears was outside, pinning a notice to the wall:

"A PENNY FOR THE GUY! COME AND SEE THIS
MARVELLOUS LIFE-SIZE DUMMY!"

Poor Grey Ears, meanwhile, got dressed . . . .
"Wow, Grey Ears, you look great!" grinned Brown Ears when he

came back into the shop. "Now just keep your head down so that no one recognises you, and for goodness sake keep absolutely still! You make a magnificent Guy, you know!"

Grey Ears grunted and settled down as comfortably as he possibly could on the hard wooden seat.

He felt a little foolish dressed up in these old clothes. He also felt very hot and itchy! Why did he always get the difficult or uncomfortable jobs when Brown Ears was carrying out his wild ideas? It wasn't fair, really it wasn't! He wriggled a little and scratched his nose.

"*Sit still!*" repeated Brown Ears in a loud whisper.

It did not take long for Brown Ears' notice to draw the attention of passers-by. Everybody who read it wanted to see this wonderful Guy, and came into the shop. "What a life-like model!" they all said. "How real he looks – almost alive!"

Before many minutes had passed, Grey Ears had quite a collection of coins at his feet.   Brown Ears gathered them up and put them in his pocket.

"Can I stand up now?" asked Grey Ears.

"No, no!   Not yet!" insisted Brown Ears.   "This is going really well! Even better than I expected!"

Grey Ears settled down reluctantly once more.

All afternoon, people kept popping in to look at him, and bit by bit the two rabbits collected quite a lot of money.

"Terrific! Wonderful! Lots of lovely loot!" Brown Ears was over the moon.

Eagerly he began planning what sort of fireworks they would buy with all their money when they had finished work later that afternoon.

"Rockets, Grey Ears, don't you think?   Lots of rockets!   I do so love to watch them go whizzing up into the air, and then *Swoosh! Bang!*" His paws waved wildly in the air.

"And we'll have some sparklers to hold, to write our names in the sky with!" he continued, rubbing his paws together with glee.   "Oh! And what are those ones that go round and round called?"

"Catherine wheels," said Grey Ears flatly.

"And just think, Grey Ears, we'll have all those humbugs to suck while we watch the display!" Brown Ears was so happy he felt like jumping for joy.

Grey Ears was not nearly so happy, however. It was all very well to have people admiring him, but some of the things that they were saying were making him feel distinctly uneasy. "I'm really looking forward to seeing that Guy burning on top of the bonfire!" they would say, or, "What a sight he'll make when he burns tonight!"

The very thought of it made Grey Ears tremble – he was glad that he wasn't a *real* Guy!

And then Drew the Shrew and Mrs Hare came in to have a look, and things began to go seriously wrong. Mrs Hare ordered herself a pound and a half of treacle toffees, and while Brown Ears was weighing them out behind the counter, she turned to give Grey Ears a proper inspection.

"My, oh my, that is the best-looking Guy Fawkes that I have ever seen in my whole life!" she declared. Grey Ears tried to keep still and not to sigh. He had heard all this before and was really rather bored with it all.

Drew the Shrew nodded in agreement. Then came the bit that Grey Ears didn't like to hear: "He's going to make a fine display, sitting on top of the bonfire with fireworks going off all around him!" Nevertheless, Grey Ears kept calm and remained as still as a statue.

But wait – what was Drew the Shrew saying now? "It must have taken you a very long time to build such a big Guy – he really is life-size isn't he? How heavy is he? I'll bet he weighs a ton!" Brown Ears was nodding and agreeing and weighing out the treacle toffees . . . . Drew the Shrew went on: "You're going to have an awful lot of trouble carrying that great monster all the way to the top of the fire, you know!"

Brown Ears nodded. "Yes, yes, I suppose I am," he said. Grey Ears held his breath. He had a horrible feeling that he knew what was going to happen next. It was Mrs Hare's turn to speak; "What we should do is gather a few more people together and do the job now. Brown Ears can't do anything while he's working this afternoon, and it's bonfire time as soon as it gets dark!"

Grey Ears could feel himself beginning to tremble. Things were sounding very bad, very bad indeed! Why didn't Brown Ears do something to help him out?

And then . . . "Oh look!" cried Drew. "There are Bill Badger and Ricky Raccoon coming along the street ! Let's get them to help us put the Guy on the bonfire now!"

Grey Ears panicked. He jumped up from his seat, screaming.

"No! I'm not going on the bonfire! You can't do this to me! I'm not a dummy!"

Poor Mrs Hare just about jumped out of her skin. Drew the Shrew turned to Brown Ears for an explanation, but Brown Ears was up and running out of the shop already. "Come on, Grey Ears!" he called. "Let's get out of here!"

And so it was that the two rabbits spent Bonfire Night at home – no food in the cupboards (their pile of money having been left behind when they fled from Sam's shop) and certainly no fireworks or humbugs from Sam, who was very cross indeed!

Grey Rabbit sat in his chair and sighed. "Well, Brown Ears, I've learned my lesson. I shall never, ever listen to you and your silly ideas again. Never!"

Brown Ears didn't believe him.

Do you?

Chimney Sweeps
And Trouble

Brown Ears was hiding behind a tree watching Mr Badger take a
snooze after his chimney-sweeping work. He was longing to tell his
friend Grey Ears about him so he scuttled off home.

"Hello, Grey Ears!" he shouted. "Come on! Look out of the window and I'll show you something very interesting."

"I can only see Mr Piglet, Mr Mouse and Mrs Turtle walking down the street," said his friend.

"Wait a moment.   Be patient, he'll soon be here!" said Brown Ears, adding, "There goes Mr Badger! He's carrying his tools on his shoulder."

"So, what has Mr Badger got to do with us?"

"Well, a lot! Because we're going to do his job."

"What? Us? But we don't know anything about cleaning chimneys," said Grey Ears who was shocked by his friend's latest idea.

The rabbits were a crafty pair; with their clever and cheeky chatter they had managed to convince the whole of Whiskerton to provide for them without having to lift a finger.

However, it was becoming more and more difficult to trick the villagers, and their endless pranks really were a nuisance.

That day, as usual, they were outdoors looking for adventure but had not found it.   As their tummies were now rumbling, a new idea occurred to Brown Ears, who said:

"It's easy work.   I've seen him sleeping like a log."

"Did you say work?" replied Grey Ears.   "But work frightens you!"

"This will be easy.   You'll see! Tomorrow, when Mr Badger is having his daily snooze, we'll borrow his tools and earn some money. Then we'll put them back where they were, and when he wakes up, he won't be any the wiser."

The next day they did as Brown Ears had said and went through Whiskerton's streets, shouting, "Chimney sweep! Chimney sweep!"

Suddenly, Grey Ears said to his friend:

"What will happen if Mr Badger wakes up and finds his tools have gone?"

"Bah!" said Brown Ears.   "He's such a sleepy head he'll spend the rest of the day trying to remember where he left them."

"Do you really think it's going to be so easy?" repeated Grey Ears.

"Mark my words," answered Brown Ears.

"No, you mark mine, but for now let's see how we go!"

"It won't fail this time.   You can't deny it's a brilliant idea."

Brown Ears kept on calling, "Chimney sweeeeeep!"

Mrs Squirrel heard his cry and looked out of the window.   She saw them and called:

"Gracious! What a surprise! Have you two decided to get a job?"

"Do you need us to sweep your chimney, Mrs Squirrel?" asked Grey Ears very politely.

"I don't know whether I can trust you.   Can you really clean chimneys?"

"Of course! Let us do the job!" Brown Ears quickly replied.

Brown Ears and Grey Ears went into Mrs Squirrel's house and through to the kitchen.

They went wild with joy!   There on the table was a large steaming loaf.   It was fresh out of the oven and smelt delicious.

In the pantry they could see a large chocolate cake covered with red cherries, and on a small shelf there was a basket full of shiny apples.

Mrs Squirrel was rather short-sighted and had not noticed how jittery the two rabbits were.   She told them how she had lit the oven that morning to bake some bread and how there was smoke everywhere.   Something must be broken.

Brown Ears had a good look and realised that Mrs Squirrel had forgotten to open the small oven door.   It would be easy, but ...

"Dear me!" said Brown Ears. "This is not going to be easy.   It could take a long time."

Grey Ears, who had also realised that they only needed to open the oven door, was confused, but he quickly guessed his friend's scheme and said:

"Yes, yes.   It's one of the most difficult faults there is."

"Hmm! We'll have to light the living-room fire to see where the smoke comes out," said Brown Ears, wrinkling his nose.

They lit an enormous fire, and after a little while Mrs Squirrel shrieked, "Oh! I can't stand this heat! While you're repairing the fault I'll slip round to visit my friend Mrs Magpie."

Off Mrs Squirrel went, and our two friends rushed into the kitchen. At last they could fill their empty tummies!

When they had eaten their fill, they happily looked at each other and burst out laughing.

"All we have to do now is open the little oven door and put out the living-room fire," said Brown Ears.

When Mrs Squirrel returned and went into the kitchen, she thought a whirlwind had passed through it. Most of her baking was gone, and her apple basket was nearly empty. She put on her glasses to look at the note lying on the table. It read:

"It was a difficult job and we were so tired and hungry that we ate a little of your food. You do not need to reward us, you are such a good cook that we feel well paid."

Brown Ears and Grey Ears were on their way home when Mimi Badger called them.

"Hey, you two! I want you to repair the kitchen chimney for me."

"What a nuisance," thought the rabbits. They wanted to go home for a snooze.

"Sorry, but we're expected somewhere else," called Brown Ears.

But Mimi, who could be very bad-tempered, stood in front of them and blocked their way.

"This job is urgent! If you don't do something to stop my chimney smoking, I shall have to send for the firemen."

Our two friends had little choice but to do as Mimi wanted. When they looked inside the kitchen, they were shocked to see that it could not be fixed as easily as Mrs Squirrel's.

"Do we know how to fix it?" whispered Grey Ears to his friend.

"Shut up!" Brown Ears quickly answered. "Don't let Mimi hear you. Look busy!"

They did the job quickly and clumsily, showering clouds of soot over the cooking pot.

"Quick, Grey Ears! There's something blocking it up, and the brooms aren't long enough to reach it. You'll have to squeeze in and squeeze out at the other end, through the living-room fireplace."

Grey Ears almost fainted when he heard those words.

From inside the chimney, Brown Ears could hear:

"What's this? Thank goodness! I've found the blockage. It's a loose brick."

"Grab it and come down. Don't waste time!" shouted Brown Ears.

Grey Ears shot down the chimney so fast that he landed in a huge pile of soot in the middle of the carpet.

"What will Mimi say when she sees this mess?" squeaked Brown
Ears. "And she's got such a bad temper!"

But our two friends did not wait to hear what Mimi had to say.
They ran out of the house and hid up on the rooftop.

But they couldn't stay there all day, so when they spotted Mimi on her way home, they quickly climbed down from the rooftop and ran away.

The two rabbits ran past Mr Cockerel and Mr Fox.   They both
looked disapprovingly at Brown Ears and Grey Ears and guessed that
the two rabbits had been playing another trick.

When Mimi saw what a mess Brown Ears and Grey Ears had made on her new carpet and how all the crockery was covered in a thick layer of soot, she was very annoyed.

Poor Mimi didn't know where to start. There was so much cleaning up to do, and her husband was due home at any moment, and the two rabbits had ruined the dinner. They really were a pair of rascals. Mimi thought that they should be punished for the damage they had caused.

When Mimi's husband arrived home, he tried to console her and helped wash the crockery and sweep the carpet.

"Don't worry, darling. You'll see how everything will turn out right in the end."

"Yes, yes, but who'll clean up the house?"

Meanwhile, our two friends were safely back home.

"We're well out of that!" squeaked Brown Ears, mopping away the sweat from his brow.

"I'm a real mess!" said Brown Ears, looking at his soot-covered

clothes. "Ha! Ha! Ha!" laughed Brown Ears, looking at his friend.

"Don't you laugh at me! You don't look too good either!"

"All right! Don't get upset, Grey Ears! Thank goodness we got away from the Badgers, without getting our tails burnt."

Everybody in Whiskerton had been fooled by the rabbits' tricks and jokes, but Mimi decided it was high time to call in the police, to teach them a lesson.

Luckily for them, Mrs Squirrel said that her own oven was working better than ever since they had repaired it.

"This time," warned Constable Weasel, "I'm not going to lock you up, but as punishment you must clean Mimi's house."

Mimi decided to make them clean out the coal cellar. She hated it because it was such a dirty job.

That evening, while they washed and combed their whiskers, Grey Ears complained:

"I'm fed up with your ideas!   Everything always ends up like this!" he said, scrubbing his dirty hands.

"All right! All right! It could have been worse.   At least it was only a dirty job!   I'll think of a better idea tomorrow!"

And he probably will!

Rabbits Run Riot!

Best Friends Do Have Birthdays

It was late at night, and Grey Ears and Brown Ears were in bed, but
Grey Ears was having trouble getting to sleep. He was looking very
gloomy, and every now and then he heaved a great big sigh.

"Whatever is the matter, Grey Ears ?" asked Brown Ears. "I can't
get to sleep with all your huffing and puffing."

Grey Ears heaved another enormous sigh, was silent for a moment,
and then said glumly "It's my birthday tomorrow."

"Your birthday? So it is! I almost forgot! But that's a nice thing to think about, isn't it, so why are you so miserable?"

"Oh well, I don't expect anybody will remember, that's all. Everybody's always so cross with us that they won't care whether or not it's my birthday." A tear gleamed in his eye and his whiskers drooped.

"Cheer up, Grey Ears, please!" urged his friend. "We'll have a little birthday celebration all of our own.   It'll be lovely!"

"How can we have a celebration when we have no money or nice food?" asked poor Grey Ears, choking back a sob.

"Tomorrow we will go out and do some nice odd jobs for some of the villagers, then we will buy food with the money we earn, and make you a special birthday supper. Don't worry, it will be a birthday to remember! Now, go to sleep and get a good rest before your special day."   And with that Brown Ears gave his friend a big hug and the two rabbits settled down for the night.   Grey Ears, by now much comforted, went straight to sleep.   But Brown Ears lay awake for some time - he was making a very special plan!

Brown Ears could be called many bad things at times. He could be called selfish, dishonest, wicked, scheming and untrustworthy, for at times he was all of those things.   But, at heart, Brown Ears was really quite a kind rabbit, and his very best friend, Grey Ears, was about to find out just how kind Brown Ears could be!

158

Next morning, bright and early, Brown Ears got up. "You stay in bed a while longer, Grey Ears. You deserve a long lie-in on your birthday."

Grey Ears snuggled down and Brown Ears set to work.

Within a short time he had several of the villagers gathered together, and he told them of his plan.

"I know you are often very angry with Grey Ears and myself," he

said to them, "for we do get up to a lot of mischief, but most of the time it's really all my fault, for I have the ideas for all our tricks – he just goes along with whatever I say.

"And now it's his birthday, and he thinks everyone has forgotten. I want to give him the best surprise ever. Will you help?"

The villagers nodded.

"Okay," said Brown Ears and whispered, "This is what we'll do . . . ."

After everyone had agreed their part in the grand surprise, they all went off, and Brown Ears went home to wake his friend.

"Come on, Grey Ears. Time to get to work! We want money for a special supper tonight, remember! Let's start by finding if there's anything we can do for Uncle Ronald !" The two rabbits set off.

They arrived at Uncle Ronald's to find him harvesting carrots from his garden.   He gave the friends a drink of water, but wouldn't let them touch the carrots.

"Get your teeth off that carrot, Brown Ears!" he said sternly.   "These are all for Mrs Mole.   She's doing some cooking today for a special occasion."

"Oh, how exciting!   What is it?" asked Grey Ears.

"Nothing that concerns you two !" retorted Uncle Ronald.

Grey Ears did not notice, but Uncle Ronald winked at Brown Ears as he said this.   He was in on the surprise.

"Now why don't you both take these to Mrs Mole's for me?" he continued.

Grey Ears and Brown Ears gathered up the carrots and were just about to leave when Uncle Ronald said, "I'm sorry I can't pay you for this job, I haven't any money today.   Never mind, eh!" and he waved them off.

"So much for our first odd job!" grumbled Grey Ears as they humped the bags of carrots along the road.

"Never mind, Grey Ears!" said Brown Ear.   "Perhaps Mrs Mole has something for us to do!"

Grey Ears might have felt a little depressed at this setback, but Brown Ears, on the other hand, was secretly delighted.   His plan, the best plan he had had for a very long time, was working beautifully!   If everybody followed instructions in the same way as Uncle Ronald had done, everything would be absolutely perfect!   Unseen by Grey Ears he gave a little hop and a skip, nearly dropping his carrots as he did so!

Well, did Mrs. Mole have any work for our friends?

She certainly had! "Odd jobs? I've so many jobs to do I could keep you busy all day!" she said. "And you can start by peeling all those carrots!" A lovely aroma of vegetable stew wafted over from Mrs Mole's cooker as the two rabbits sat down to their task. Grey Ears wrinkled up his nose. He was hungry and the smell was just torture!

If he could choose just one special thing he would like for his birthday, it would be a plate of Mrs Mole's famous vegetable stew. . . .

"Of course I won't be able to pay you until tomorrow!" said Mrs Mole, standing over the cooker so that Grey Ears wouldn't see the secret smile on her face. "You can wait, can't you ?"

"Come on, let's get out of here!" whispered Grey Ears. "We'll never earn any money at this rate!"

He waited until he was sure that Mrs Mole wasn't looking, then nudged Brown Ears and urged him out of the kitchen after him. Brown Ears smiled to himself. Everything was going perfectly according to plan!

"Let's try Harry Hedgehog next!" he suggested merrily.

They found Harry Hedgehog, like Uncle Ronald, working in his
garden.   He had been gathering bunches of flowers.

"Need something to do, eh?" he grunted at them.   "Well, you can
take these flowers over to Mrs Mole's for me.   She must be having a bit
of a do this evening."

"She is indeed!" Grey Ears said as the rabbits took the flowers from
Harry.   "Goodness knows what she's up to.   But thank you for giving
us the job anyway.   We're needing to earn a little money you see . . . ."

"Oh, I'm not going to pay you!" said Harry.   "You two owe me a
favour or two after all.   You can do this free of charge!"

Without a word, Grey Ears thrust the flowers back at Harry Hedgehog and stormed off. Brown Ears did the same, but not before he and Harry had exchanged knowing winks. Grey Ears was getting more and more distressed, but trying hard not to show it. "This isn't working out!" he said. "Not working out at all! If we go on like this, we'll end up with nothing for my birthday tea!" Brown Ears patted his head comfortingly. "Cheer up, old friend. We musn't give up hope yet!"

All day long Brown Ears and Grey Ears tramped the streets of Whiskerton. Brown Ears led his friend here, there and everywhere in their search for paid work. Everywhere they went, they were offered jobs to do, but everybody, for different reasons, refused to pay them for what they did. Grey Ears was exhausted, hungry and in despair.

"Come on, Brown Ears," he said, "I've had enough of this. It's nearly dark, and we're both tired out. Let's just go home."

He looked hard at Brown Ears. For some reason, in spite of the awful day they had had, Brown Ears appeared remarkably cheerful. Grey Ears just couldn't understand it! Brown Ears put his arm round his friend's shoulders.

"Very well, Grey Ears," he agreed. "I can see how tired you are. Perhaps we should give up. But don't despair, we can still have a good time. I found some old lettuce left from last week in the cupboard this morning. I'll boil up some soup with it and we'll light a candle to celebrate!"

Grey Ears shrugged his shoulders miserably. Last week's lettuce! Ugh! The two friends set off for home.

Brown Ears bounded on ahead while Grey Ears trudged slowly along the road, fighting back the tears of disappointment. Brown Ears had certainly tried hard, he thought, but it looked as if a miserable birthday evening lay ahead.

Brown Ears, on the other hand, knew different!

By the time they got home it was almost dark.

"Don't be downhearted, my friend!" insisted Brown Ears. "You go straight through to the bedroom and change into your best suit! It is your birthday after all!"

Grey Ears gritted his teeth but said nothing, and as Brown Ears opened the door he went gloomily through to the bedroom.   Brown Ears followed Grey Ears, quickly changed into his best clothes also, then hurried into the living room ahead of his friend.

Grey Ears wearily tied his tie, then plodded through to the living room.

"*Surprise*! *Happy birthday*!"

Grey Ears could not believe his eyes.   There in the sitting room was Brown Ears, and all round him were the villagers who had tried to make them work for nothing that day!   And what was that he could smell? Mrs Mole's vegetable stew! And Harry Hedgehog's flowers were all around the room!   The fire was lit and the room looked welcoming.

"I bet you never expected this, did you?" beamed Brown Ears. "I bet you thought that everybody had forgotten!   It was all part of our plan!" Grey Ears was speechless.   The worst possible kind of day had turned into the best possible kind of day.

"I do hope you're hungry!" beamed Mrs Mole   "I've made all your favourite food!"

Grey Ears nodded dumbly.

"I hope you're going to eat plenty, m'boy" boomed Uncle Ronald jovially.   "Remember my best vegetables are in that stew !"

Grey Ears had to pinch himself in case he was dreaming!

"Nothing but the best for my very best friend on his special day!" Brown Ears gazed fondly at Grey Ears.   Grey Ears blushed. Everybody clapped.

"What are we all waiting for, then?" called Brown Ears.   "Let's tuck in!"

Later, after several plates of vegetable stew, several slices of carrot cake and lots of jolly party games, Grey Ears made a small speech.

"I want to thank you all for the wonderful surprise," he said. "I must admit you all had me fooled. You have all worked so hard to make this a wonderful birthday, and I shall never forget your kindness. Thank you!" He paused, then spoke again:

"Oh – Brown Ears – this was the best idea you have ever had!"

Cross My Palm
With Silver

Grey Ears and Brown Ears were up in their bedroom one morning admiring Grey Ears in the mirror.   He was looking unusually smart.

    He had on his best striped trousers and a tail coat, a beautiful bow tie, big shiny boots and, as a final flamboyant touch, a large floppy top hat with a feather in it.

"You'll do," said Brown Ears, satisfied at last.

"Do for what exactly, Brown Ears ?" asked Grey Ears, puzzled. He couldn't think why on earth his friend had dressed him up like this, even if he was rather pleased with his appearance himself.

"Oh, not much really just a spot of advertising," said Brown Ears.

"Advertising?" Grey Ears was none the wiser.

"Well," said Brown Ears proudly, "I have a plan . . . ."

Grey Ears felt his heart sinking into his big shiny boots. He always felt that way when Brown Ears said those four awful words: "I have a plan . . . ." Oh dear !

"Um – Brown Ears" he said with trepidation, "just exactly what is your plan?"

"Oh don't concern yourself, my dear chap," said Brown Ears airily. "It's all perfectly simple. No problem at all. We'll be rich after tomorrow! Now, first things first. Repeat after me, "My Uncle Aloysius . . . ."

"But I don't have an uncle Aloysius!" protested Grey Ears.

"I know that, and you know that, but does anybody else know that?" said Brown Ears. "I don't think so. Now, come on, Grey Ears, my Uncle Aloysius, the famous fortune teller, is coming to town . . . ."

Slowly they proceeded with Grey Ears' lesson until he was word perfect, and then Brown Ears explained his latest plan to his friend . . ..

Some time later Grey Ears set off along the road to the village.   As
he went, he kept repeating his lines to himself to help him to
remember.   "My Uncle Aloysius, the great fortune teller . . . , My Uncle
Aloysius, the great fortune teller . . ."

When he reached the village, Grey Ears set to work. Brown Ears would have been proud of him had he seen him in action. Everywhere he went, he stopped people and engaged them in conversation.

"My Uncle Aloysius, the great fortune teller – perhaps you've heard of him – oh, you haven't? Well, anyway, my Uncle Aloysius is a great fortune teller, renowned throughout the country for the accuracy of his predictions and the wisdom of his advice. He travels from town to town, thrilling all who come to see him with his astonishing performance. And now he has written to me to tell me that he intends to come here to offer his fortune-telling services to all of you here. I am to be his assistant – isn't that exciting? He's only going to be here for one day, so if you want to see him you'd better be sure to come tomorrow!"

Everywhere Grey Ears went he stirred up great excitement with his news, and before long the High Street was buzzing with the chatter of villagers eager to go and see this famous man.

It may seem strange to you, but not one of these villagers wondered why Grey Ears had never mentioned this famous uncle to them before.

No one, that is, until Brown Ears' cousin, Richard Rabbit, appeared and overhead Grey Ears. He knew Grey Ears didn't have an Uncle Aloysius. He sneaked off, unseen by Grey Ears, for a chat with Constable Weasel . . . .

Next morning, bright and early, the two rascals were once again to be found in front of their bedroom mirror.   Brown Ears had made himself a magnificent cape from an old pair of curtains and a very magical looking starry hat.   He really looked the part – he was Aloysius, the fortune teller !   Brown Ears felt a little foolish in the frilly shirt and velvet waistband that Brown Ears had made him put on, but when Brown Ears assured him that he looked absolutely perfect for his job as assistant to the fortune teller, he felt slightly better.

Brown Ears gave one final adjustment to his cape and then beckoned to his friend, "Come on, Grey Ears, let's get that tent up before the villagers start to arrive."

They had scarcely finished when Harry Hedgehog appeared.　He could hardly contain his excitement.

"It is an honour to meet you, sir, em, your grace, um, your highness Aloysius!" he gasped, bowing low.　"It's strange, though, I feel as if I've seen you somewhere before!"

Grey Ears realised what was happening.

"Quick, Brown Ears, into the tent before he recognises you!　It's darker in there!" he whispered.

"If you'll just follow me, sir . . ." he said to Harry.

Safely inside the darkness of the tent, with his friend disguised in the shadows of the curtains where he was less likely to be recognised, Grey Ears relaxed a little bit. He even began to enjoy himself. Brown Ears, it turned out, was surprisingly good at fake fortune telling, and listening to him with Harry Hedgehog for his first client made some good entertainment.

"You don't even have to tell me your name, my good sir," began Brown Ears, "because my magic powers are already telling me what it is! Now, let me see, it begins with 'H'. Wait a minute, it's clearer to me now; it's Harry, isn't it?"

Harry was amazed! How could this stranger know his name? Little did he know that it wasn't a stranger at all!

"Now, Harry, about my fee . . ." continued Brown Ears. Without hesitation, Harry produced his purse.

"I don't personally deal with money at all – too vulgar, don't you know," said Brown Ears, "but if you'll pass three silver coins to my assistant, Grey Ears – yes, that's right, that's it!"

Grey Ears could hardly believe his eyes as Harry meekly handed over the money. *Three silver coins*! To Grey Ears, who hardly ever had money, it was a fortune!

Brown Ears settled himself more comfortably in his seat, took Harry Hedgehog's little paw in his, and began his consultation . . . .

"I can see a great future ahead of you, Harry, as a cultivator of delicious foodstuffs," said Brown Ears. "You have a gift for growing things. Keep it up, share your produce with others, and great things will happen to you."

Well, Harry Hedgehog liked nothing better than pottering about in his allotment, growing cabbages and carrots and other vegetables. He was quite good at it too (as Brown Ears and Grey Ears could both testify, having stolen many a lettuce or pea pod from him in the past!), so to be told by a fortune teller, as great as he believed this one to be, that it would profit him to continue delighted him!

Brown Ears went on: "You are going to meet a beautiful hedgehog called Henrietta, who will make you very happy, and you will marry her." Harry Hedgehog blushed. "I see great riches and a contented life ahead of you. I see that you have worked hard all your life and deserve the wealth you will acquire, but never forget those who are less fortunate than yourself, especially rabbits!" Grey Ears tried not to giggle. Not only was Brown Ears making money from Harry, but he was also ensuring a good supply of vegetables for himself in the future!

By the time Brown Ears had finished, Harry was so deliriously happy that he could hardly speak!

"Th-thank you, y-your um f-fortune tellership," he gasped, bowing low.

"No trouble!" said Brown Ears with a wave of his paw as Harry Hedgehog stumbled backwards out of the tent, bowing and scraping as he went.

"That was fun!" said Brown Ears after he had gone. "Now who's next, I wonder?" He turned towards the doorway to see Mr Badger striding in, trying to appear calm but really rather nervous, all dressed in his best clothes, eager to hear what lay ahead of him in his life.

Brown Ears made an excellent job of telling Mr Badger's future. Just as he had done with Harry Hedgehog, Brown Ears promised that wonderful things would happen to Mr Badger. Mr Badger could hardly prevent himself from jumping for joy when he heard all that Brown Ears had to tell him. Mr Badger, you see, was not a wealthy man at all. He worked very hard indeed, sweeping chimneys for a living, but he didn't really earn very much money at all. He found it quite a struggle to make ends meet, especially as he had four hungry baby badgers growing fast to feed! Brown Ears told him that he was going to find buried treasure, which would make him very rich, and he would be able to buy a big house for himself and his family, and have plenty of money left to keep himself and his family well fed and comfortable for the rest of their lives.

Brown Ears, in fact, got rather carried away. He didn't stop to think that promising such things to Mr Badger was really very unkind, when he knew perfectly well that they were highly unlikely to happen. He didn't think that Mr Badger might waste the rest of his life searching for buried treasure that did not exist, waiting for wealth that was never going to come to him. Brown Ears was so involved in making up his amazing stories that the thought of all the unhappiness he might be causing simply never occurred to him.

He was, in fact, telling whopping great lies, and lies cause nothing but trouble, as we all know, but Brown Ears just was not thinking.

Mr Badger left, and Mrs Mouse immediately came in. She was so completely overawed by the appearance of the fortune teller and by all that she had heard about him that she stood open-mouthed and speechless for most of her consultation with Brown Ears. In fact, it did not seem to Grey Ears that she was listening to much of what Brown Ears was saying as she stared at him with eyes glazed, mouth agape. Nevertheless, she was happy when she left, and Brown Ears was particularly pleased with the nonsense that he had told her!

It seemed that nothing could go wrong with Brown Ears' latest wheeze.   Everything was going perfectly – or was it?

Remember Brown Ears' cousin Richard?   Shouldn't we find out what happened when he went to see Constable Weasel?

Constable Weasel was very interested to hear what Richard Rabbit had to tell him.

"Uncle Aloysius, eh? And you say that Grey Ears has not got an Uncle Aloysius ?" Constable Weasel's brain was ticking over very fast!

"Yes, sir, that is correct.   I know for a fact that Grey Ears only has one uncle, Uncle Raymond that is!"

"And was Brown Ears anywhere to be seen while Grey Ears was telling this fairy story about – um – Uncle Aloysius ?" Constable Weasel was beginning to work things out.

"No, sir, he was not!" said Richard importantly.

"I think perhaps I'll call round and see this mysterious fortune teller at work – tomorrow did you say?" Constable Weasel was now on the trail!

So, while Brown Ears and Grey Ears were happily playing fortune telling, believing things were going swimmingly well, Constable Weasel, unknown to them, was on his way.

And while Grey Ears and Brown Ears were waving goodbye to Mrs Mouse, Constable Weasel, still unknown to them, was outside the tent, gathering evidence from Mr Badger and Harry Hedgehog, who couldn't understand why on earth Constable Weasel was asking so many questions about the great Aloysius!

Once Mrs Mouse had gone, Brown Ears and Grey Ears wondered why nobody else was coming in.   And then they heard Constable Weasel's voice, and their hearts sank! What was he doing there?

Constable Weasel, convinced that he knew what sort of trouble was up, was now striding into the tent.

Bemused and perplexed, Mr Badger, Mrs Mouse and Harry
Hedgehog followed in behind.   Grey Ears gulped, panic-stricken.

It looked for a moment as if Brown Ears was going to get away with
it.   It looked for a moment as if Constable Weasel, too, had been taken
in by the great Aloysius.   Meekly, it seemed, Constable Weasel held
out his paw to be read by the fake fortune teller.   Brown Ears, thinking
that Constable Weasel had not recognised him, launched into his
introductory speech: "Good sir, you do not have to tell me your
name . . . ."

"Because you know it already, *Brown Ears*!" growled Constable
Weasel.

The game was up. Our two pranksters had been caught in the act, thanks to Richard Rabbit and Constable Weasel.

"Up to your tricks again, eh, Brown Ears?" said Constable Weasel as he eyed the two rabbits sternly. "Well, let me tell you that you could be in for a lot of trouble this time! Let's see now . . . pretending to be someone else in order to extract money from other people . . . in legal circles we call that fraud! A very serious crime indeed! And have you got a licence for this business of yours? I think not! That is another serious offence, you know!"

"Oh, Constable Weasel, we didn't mean any harm, you know, honestly we didn't!" squeaked Brown Ears.

Grey Ears kept his mouth firmly shut. He didn't want to say anything in case he got himself into further trouble! Brown Ears continued, "It was no more than a harmless joke, really it was! We weren't really going to keep any of the money that we were paid! Surely you didn't think we would do such a thing! Certainly not!"

Grey Ears could not believe that Brown Ears would tell such awful fibs so easily – but Brown Ears was desperate to save his skin !

"We have the money safe here, and we were going to give it back at the end of the day – weren't we, Grey Ears ?" Grey Ears nodded dumbly.

"And as for the licence . . . well, my dear Constable Weasel, had we only known we were supposed to have one, I can assure you we would have got one and pinned it on the door for all to see!"

Constable Weasel waved a paw to stop Brown Ears saying any more. "I should put you two in jail for this," he said, "but the thought of Brown Ears gibbering on like this all night is enough to drive me mad! You must give back the money that you were paid for this ridiculous farce, but apart from that, I shall be lenient and let you off this time. But *next* time . . ." he snarled menacingly at the two rabbits, and they knew exactly what he meant!

Outside the tent, Brown Ears was almost glad to give the money back to Mr Badger, Harry Hedgehog and Mrs Mouse. Anything rather than face a spell in a prison cell!

Grey Ears sighed. All that work and nothing to show for it but trouble: Why oh, why, did he have to get himself involved in Brown Ears' crazy schemes? Gloomily he turned his thoughts to their empty larder at home. No food, no money. It was going to be another hungry night, thanks to Brown Ears!

Postal Panic

Grey Ears was happy. It looked like being a good day. He and
Brown Ears had food in the cupboards for a change, and were enjoying
a very peaceful breakfast. Brown Ears had been on his best behaviour
lately, and even seemed to be enjoying being good.

Then a letter came under the door. The two rabbits' ears pricked
up. Who could it be from?

They rushed to pick it up and looked at the writing on the envelope.

"Wait a minute, Grey Ears!" exclaimed Brown Ears. "This is not for us! It's addressed to Dr Squirrel! I wonder who's writing to him? I wonder what it says ? Perhaps it's something exciting!"

Brown Ears was just about to open the letter and have a look when Grey Ears stopped him.

"You musn't do that, Brown Ears!" he cried. "It is wrong to read other people's letters. In fact, it's against the law!"

"We could always pretend that we opened it by mistake," suggested Brown Ears.

"We certainly could not, Brown Ears," said his friend crossly. "As soon as we have finished breakfast and washed up the dishes, I'm going to take it over to Dr Squirrel's surgery, and that's that !"

"Oh, all right then," said Brown Ears huffily. "Do what you like."

After breakfast, the two rabbits set out. Brown Ears was going to do some shopping, and Grey Ears was off to the other side of the village to deliver the letter to Dr Squirrel's surgery.

Before he started his shopping, Brown Ears decided to treat himself to a dandelion soda in Mr Mouse's snack bar just nearby.

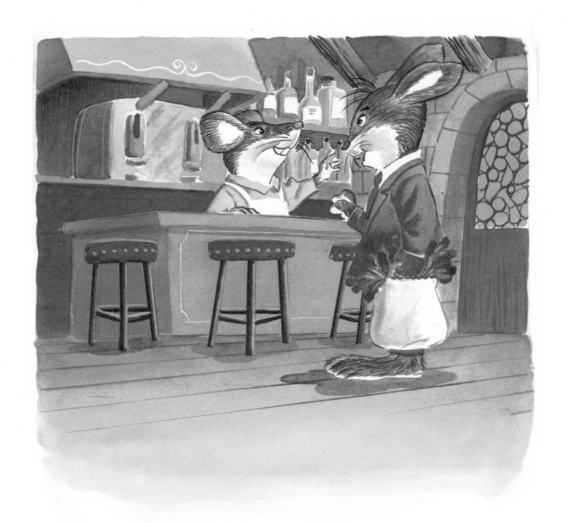

"Do you know, Mr Mouse," he said, "that the post has been mixed up this morning?"

"Well, Brown Ears, I'm expecting a letter today, and it hasn't arrived yet. I hope it hasn't been delivered to the wrong place as well."

"Oh I shouldn't be surprised if it has," said Brown Ears airily, and he left the shop.

Now, when there was trouble in Whiskerton, Brown Ears and Grey Ears often had something to do with it. And whether or not they did have something to with it, they were always the first to come under suspicion. Brown Ears' news had made Mr Mouse suspicious already!

Brown Ears should have kept quiet. Minutes later, Mabel Mouse
was outside the snack bar talking to Sam Squirrel, the bank clerk.

"The post for the village has been all mixed up!" she exclaimed "And
Brown Ears and Grey Ears know something about it! I bet they've
been up to nonsense again!"

"You're probably right," agreed Sam. "Those two have been good
for too long!"

Brown Ears' innocent remarks had sparked off a rumour which was
now flying round the village!

Grey Ears, meanwhile, had reached Dr Squirrel's house, and was
reading a note which Dr Squirrel had pinned to the door. It said:
"Have gone out for a short while. Will all patients please leave their
names at the foot of this note and I shall call on them as soon as
possible."

"Well I'm not a patient," said Grey Ears to himself, "so I don't have
to leave my name." He put the letter through the door, and set off
home again, thinking, "I wonder where Dr Squirrel's gone anyway?"

Dr Squirrel had in fact gone into the village with a letter for Harry
Hedgehog which had been delivered to the doctor by mistake.

When he got there, he found that Harry Hedgehog had received a
letter which should have gone to Mr Badger's house. He also heard
that some of the villagers thought that Brown Ears and Grey Ears had
something to do with all this confusion. Many of the villagers had got
the wrong mail.

Wally Weasel had received a picture advertising cough sweets which had been meant for Ronald Rabbit's chemist shop. Monty Mouse was reluctantly returning an interesting parcel to Mrs Mole which had been put at his door by mistake. Did anyone have the right mail? Doctor Squirrel wondered.

"There's nothing else for it!" declared Dr Squirrel. "We must ask Constable Weasel to sort out the confusion. If the two rabbits have been mixing up all the mail, then I am sure they will be in serious trouble." Off he went to the police station with Harry Hedgehog trotting along behind him, both carrying their letters as evidence.

Constable Weasel was just wondering why he had received a letter addressed to Mrs Mouse, when Dr Squirrel and Harry Hedgehog arrived at the police station.

Dr Squirrel, with several helpful interruptions from Harry Hedgehog, began to explain the problem to Constable Weasel.

As Dr Squirrel chatted on, Constable Weasel's face grew more and more grim. In the past he had wasted a lot of valuable police time sorting out the confusion and consternation caused by the antics of Grey Ears and Brown Ears. Those rabbits really were an infernal nuisance, and now it looked as if they were up to more nonsense. It made Constable Weasel so angry!

"So that's it!" exclaimed Constable Weasel when he had heard Dr Squirrel's story. "It probably is another monstrous trick played by those dreadful rabbits. They will have to be brought in for questioning. But first we must inform Mrs Duck at the Post Office that someone has been tampering with the mail."

The three of them left the police station and made their way to the Post Office.

Brown Ears had just finished the shopping and was sitting in the sunshine rewarding himself with a small snack of carrots when Roly Racoon rushed up to him.   "Better beat it quick, Brown Ears! Constable Weasel is after you!"

"But I haven't done anything wrong!" spluttered Brown Ears, spitting carrot all over the pavement.

"He thinks you have, and he's coming to get you!"

Without hesitation, Brown Ears beetled off home to find Grey Ears.

Meanwhile Constable
Weasel, Dr Squirrel and
Harry Hedgehog had
arrived at the Post Office
and were surprised to find
that it was closed.

"I'll go round the back
to see if I can find
anyone," said Constable
Weasel.

Dr Squirrel stayed by
the front door, ringing the
bell and calling, "Hello!
Anyone in there?"

After a few minutes Mrs
Duck popped her head
out of an upstairs window.
The poor soul really
looked most unwell.

"Oh Dr Squirrel, it's you!" she croaked. "How did you know I was ill?"

"Well, actually I didn't, Mrs Duck," admitted Dr Squirrel.

"But I shall certainly examine you and see if I can help you. What I came to tell you was that the mail has been very badly mixed up today. Everybody has been getting the wrong letters. Constable Weasel thinks that Brown Ears and Grey Ears have been playing some sort of trick on us all."

"Oh no, Dr Squirrel, you mustn't blame them," Mrs Duck said hoarsely. "Let me explain. As you can see, I am not well at all, and in fact Mr Duck, who as you know usually delivers the post, is ill as well. I think it must be the flu or something. Our throats feel like sandpaper, our heads are thumping with pain, and our legs feel as if they have turned to jelly!"

Dr Squirrel nodded sympathetically. "Yes indeed, Mrs. Squirrel, flu can be very nasty, and it sounds as if you have a very nasty dose!"

Mrs Duck continued, "Well, yesterday I managed to struggle round with the letters. It took me twice as long as usual, because I was as weak as water! But even I could not manage a full delivery on my own today, so we had to have some help." She paused to clear her throat, which was very hoarse and painful-sounding, then carried on with her explanation:

"We had to borrow the postman from the next village – you know, that awful beast who charges around on his motor scooter at such a speed.   Well, he wasn't very happy at doing the extra work.   I suspect he just stuffed the letters in any old letter box without caring to whom they were addressed.   He really is a nuisance!"

Poor Grey Ears and Brown Ears, sitting at home, quaking in their boots at the thought of a visit from Constable Weasel, when they really had done nothing wrong at all!

They did not have too long to worry. As soon as the true story spread round, some of the villagers came to call on the two rabbits to tell them that it had all been a terrible mistake.

Grey Ears and Brown Ears were only too pleased to join the others and to go round to Mrs Duck's to offer help and get-well gifts. Everyone joined together to show their best wishes to the Duck family, with flowers, home cooking, get-well cards and presents. Harry Hedgehog organised a team of villagers to take over the postal deliveries and run the shop.

Mr and Mrs Duck were so delighted by the kindness which had been shown to them that as soon as they were well again they had a wonderful party to which they invited the whole village, and Grey Ears

and Brown Ears had such a good time that they forgot all about the day they had nearly been in trouble without doing anything wrong.

Crafty Art

Grey Ears and Brown Ears were at home, tidying up the house. Neither little rabbit liked doing housework and the place was in a terrible mess, so they were both feeling a bit disgruntled.

"Why are you such a messy rabbit?" Grey Ears asked Brown Ears.

"I'm not the messy one, it's you!" argued Brown Ears.

"I'm fed up!" said Grey Ears finally, and went to look out of the kitchen window. "Wait a minute!" he cried. "There's someone coming!"

Brown Ears stuck his head out of another window, and saw a fox dressed in an artist's smock approaching the house.   He was carrying some boards under his arm.   "Would you like to buy one of my paintings?" he asked, waving one up at Brown Ears.

"You stay right there, and I'll be out in a flash!" called back Brown Ears.   A plan was hatching in his head already.

This plan was going to cost him some money, but if all went according to his plan, he would be paid back at least ten times over.

"What a clever rabbit I am !" he thought to himself as he ran towards the sideboard to get his moneybox.

Brown Ears emptied out his moneybox, then Grey Ears' moneybox, and hurried to the door.   Grey Ears followed anxiously – what was Brown Ears going to do with all his money?

Grey Ears rolled his eyes in despair when he found Brown Ears eagerly handing over every penny they had to the artist, in exchange for three paintings.   What was worse, Brown Ears didn't even take a look at what he was buying!

"What on earth are you playing at, Brown Ears?" he demanded when they got back inside. "We have no food for tomorrow, and you've spent every last penny on three stupid pictures that you haven't even looked at yet! The house looks nice enough now that it has been cleaned up. It doesn't need any pictures to smarten it up!"

"Ah now," said Brown Ears. "The house doesn't need these pictures but *we* do! These pictures hold the key to our fortune! I shall tell you all about it in the morning, but now we should both get a good night's sleep. Oh – and when you get up in the morning, put on some old clothes, will you, Grey Ears?"

Poor Grey Ears went to bed, feeling puzzled to say the least!

The next morning he got up to find Brown Ears rummaging in the cellar.

"What on earth are you doing in here, Brown Ears?" he asked.

"Oh – I'm just looking for something, that's all!" panted Brown Ears, heaving an old tea chest to one side. "I know it's here somewhere, it's been here for as long as I can remember!"

"What is *it*, exactly?" enquired Grey Ears.

Brown Ears didn't answer. He just kept on searching, pausing every now and then to give an enormous sneeze. It was very dusty in the cellar.

"Go and get your oldest clothes, will you, Grey Ears?" he added as an afterthought.

Meekly Grey Ears did as he was told, while Brown Ears went on rummaging.

"Ah, I knew it was here somewhere!" he cried triumphantly as he
hauled out a creaky old invalid chair. "Try this for size, Grey Ears !"
Before Grey Ears could object, he and the paintings had been bundled
into the chair and were being pushed at breakneck speed along the
bumpy path towards the village.

"Careful, Brown Ears, you're going to trip me up at this rate!"
protested Grey Ears. "And will you please tell me what on earth is
going on?"

But try as he might, Grey Ears could not get a straight answer from his friend.

"Now, Grey Ears, all you have to do is to sit still and pretend to be ill." puffed Brown Ears as he trotted along. "Pretend to be *ill*?" shrieked Grey Ears. "Now hold on a minute, Brown Ears. I have a horrible feeling something's wrong!"

Brown Ears stopped the chair. "Something is indeed wrong, Grey Ears. We both look far too jolly in these colourful trousers. We must go back and change into more serious-looking clothes!"

"But you asked me to put on my oldest clothes!" insisted Grey Ears. "These are my oldest clothes – look, they even have holes in them!" He pointed to the elbows of his jacket, and the knees of his trousers. They were indeed threadbare, and full of holes.

"I know, I know, but they're still not right. They still don't create just the right impression. . . ." said Brown Ears.

"For *what*?" screeched Grey Ears in frustration.

But Brown Ears was off again, shoving the old invalid chair with poor Grey Ears in it as fast as he could back to the house.

"Something darker...." he muttered to himself. "More sombre. . . ."

Back at the house, the two rabbits duly got changed. "That's better! Not too well dressed, not too colourful. Sober and respectable, that's us !" exclaimed Brown Ears. Then he took a little time to explain his idea to Grey Ears before they set off again.

The plan was this: they were to go into the village to put on a show of the paintings in the street. Grey Ears was to pretend that he was seriously ill and needed lots of money for special treatment to make him better. The paintings on show were supposed to be there to earn the money which Grey Ears was pretending to need. Brown Ears was to pretend that he had painted them.

"But nobody will pay to see these paintings, Brown Ears. They're awfully ugly things!" protested Grey Ears. "Don't worry, Grey Ears," Brown Ears assured his little chum. "Everybody will be feeling so sorry for you that they won't really care what the paintings look like. They'll just give us lots of money."

"Are you sure about this?" asked Grey Ears doubtfully.

"Oh, absolutely sure!" beamed Brown Ears. "The plan is absolutely foolproof! We'll have to cover up your head, of course, to hide your healthy shiny fur, and we'll wrap a scarf around your face to disguise the fact that you look perfectly well. Oh – and you'll have to moan a little!"

Brown Ears then tried to show Grey Ears how he would write a notice on the pavement asking for donations.   But Grey Ears wasn't paying much attention to Brown Ears.   He was busy giggling at one of the paintings.

"I know that's supposed to be a carrot, but it looks to me like a portrait of Dr Squirrel with a funny hat on!" he laughed.

The two rabbits set off once more, Grey Ears still feeling unsure about the whole plot, but too well wrapped up in an enormous woolly scarf to protest any further.

"If we catch sight of Dr Squirrel, run for your life, Grey Ears!" said Brown Ears. "If he sees us, the game's up. He knows perfectly well that there's nothing wrong with you !"

Within a few minutes, the wicked pair had set up their display in the village. Brown Ears whistled merrily as he chalked on the pavement: "Please help. My friend needs money for treatment. Show your appreciation for my paintings and spare us a penny."

Grey Ears wondered if he looked ill enough.

"Where did you get that scarf, Grey Ears?" giggled Mabel Mouse.

Grey Ears was too muffled to answer.

All was quiet for a while, and then Harriet Hare came along the
street.   She wasn't very clever and had no suspicion that the two
rabbits might be up to a trick.   Without hesitation she took a coin from
her purse and put it in Brown Ears' hat.   "Good luck to both of you,"
she said kindly.

Grey Ears began to think that perhaps Brown Ears' plan might work,
especially when two more villagers came up shortly afterwards and
also gave them some money.

All the time they sat there it had been getting hotter and hotter. Grey Ears was terribly uncomfortable, but he dared not move in case his pretence was discovered, and he couldn't complain to Brown Ears because the scarf was wound so tightly round his mouth and neck that he could hardly utter a sound.

Suddenly Brown Ears jumped up. "Phew! I'm thirsty!" he announced. "I think I'll just pop along to Mr Mouse's snack bar for a nice cool drink. It's so hot out here, I feel as if I'm about to faint! Don't worry, Grey Ears, I'll be back soon!" And with that, he was off, leaving poor Grey Ears stranded there, unable to move or speak. Grey Ears sat for several minutes more, getting hotter and hotter. He closed his eyes for a minute against the glare of the sun, and within seconds he had dozed off.

While he was asleep he dreamed he was in hospital, but that it wasn't a nice hospital at all. It was a dreadfully hot place, this hospital in his dreams, and the blankets were made of hard scratchy wool (just like the woolly scarf he was wearing!), and the walls were covered with horrible, ugly pictures (just like the pictures that Brown Ears had propped up in the street beside him!). In this hospital, he had to sit on the most uncomfortable chair (just like the invalid chair he was sleeping in just now!). It really was the strangest dream.

He woke up a little while later with someone tapping on his shoulder. It was old Mrs Racoon, one of the village busybodies.

"Grey Ears! What on earth are you doing out here in the heat of the day with a fever like that! Wait here, I'm going to get some help," and off she scurried, petticoats rustling. Grey Ears could only grunt in reply. By now he was so hot he was beginning to believe that he really did have a fever. And how he wished Brown Ears hadn't found such a scratchy scarf for him to wear!

Grey Ears did not know it, but Mrs Racoon was in fact very suspicious of his "illness". She had spotted the little rabbit across the street with his friend only the day before, hopping along as perky as usual, and she knew that he could not have suddenly become as ill as he was pretending to be overnight.

She bustled off to Mrs Duck's Post Office where she found Constable Weasel's wife. Mrs Weasel knew the rabbits all too well and would be able to tell for sure if this was all a trick. Mrs Racoon explained how she had found Grey Ears, and asked Mrs Weasel to come back with her to help sort things out.

"I really don't belive he's ill at all, you see!" she said to Mrs Weasel.

"You may well be right," nodded Mrs Weasel, "and there's one sure way of finding out. Come on, let's go!" And leaving all her parcels on the counter with a very surprised Mrs Duck, she shoved Mrs Racoon back out into the street ahead of her. On the way she explained to Mrs Racoon just exactly how she intended to find out whether or not Grey Ears was pretending to be ill.

Poor Grey Ears! If he had only known that at that moment Mrs Weasel and Mrs Racoon were descending upon him, he would have leapt out of his invalid chair there and then! As it was, he just sat there, stewing in the hot sunshine.

Mrs Weasel and Mrs Racoon continued their advance.

When they reached Brown Ears, he had dozed off again. Gently Mrs Weasel rolled back a bit of the scarf covering Grey Ears' face. She saw that his nose was peeking out and could see that he was breathing quite regularly and gently.

He was certainly very hot; that much was obvious. But his fur was shiny and healthy in appearance, his nose was twitching beautifully, and there were no spots or mumps, or swollen bits to be seen. Grey Ears definitely did not look like a sick rabbit!

Mrs Weasel completed her inspection triumphantly. "This rabbit has absolutely nothing wrong with him!" she whispered softly to Mrs Racoon. "It's time we taught him a lesson. This is what we'll do. . . ." She whispered some instructions in Mrs Racoon's ear, and then winked, saying in a very loud voice:

"Oh, the poor little darling! Anyone can see he's too ill to be left out in this hot sun, and besides, he needs proper care and attention ! Mrs Racoon, your house is just around the corner, isn't it ? Let us take him there immediately and give him some treatment. I'm sure we'll have him better in next to no time!"

"What about all these lovely paintings, and the money which has been collected?" asked Mrs Racoon, equally loudly.

"Leave the paintings where they are. We'll take the money and give it away to the poor and needy. Grey Ears won't need it by the time we're finished with him!" yelled back Mrs Weasel, trying very hard not to laugh.

Grey Ears, of course, had heard all this, but was too scared to open his eyes. He thought that perhaps if he pretended still to be asleep they would leave him alone. No such luck! He was bundled and bumped along the street in that rickety old invalid chair until he felt he was black and blue all over, and then shaken and jolted into Mrs Racoon's living room, where more shocks awaited him . . . .

"Ice – and lots of it!" yelled Mrs Weasel. "Hurry, Mrs Racoon!"

Within seconds Mrs Racoon had made up an enormous ice-pack and had plonked it hard on Grey Ears' head. "Crunch," went the ice. "Oi!" screamed Grey Ears. "Don't worry, you poor little thing, we'll have you as right as rain in no time at all!" grinned Mrs Weasel. "Have you got the caster oil, Mrs Racoon?" Before Grey Ears could blink, a large dose of the horrible stuff had been poured down his throat.

Caster oil is very nasty to swallow, and even nastier when it is forced upon you. Poor Grey Ears! There was absolutely nothing he could do about it.

He sat there, choking and gasping and feeling *really* sick, while the two women bustled and fussed around him, giggling quietly to themselves.

"He's still too hot, you know," said Mrs Weasel. "Fill the bath with cold water and ice!"

That was the final straw. Grey Ears leapt out of the chair and fled from the house, leaving Mrs Weasel and Mrs Racoon laughing fit to burst.

And what of Brown Ears? What was he doing while all this was going on?

Well, he had three dandelion sodas and a large bit of carrot cake at Mr Mouse's snack bar, and was just heading back to where he had left his little friend, when Grey Ears caught up with him – and chased him all the way home!

He had to run so fast to escape his angry chum that when he got home he was very, very sick indeed, and it served him right!

The Chemist's Catastrophe

It was a lovely sunny day in Whiskerton, but Brown Ears was in a bad mood all the same. "I *hate* working !" he grumbled to Grey Ears as he drank his morning cup of dandelion coffee.

"Cheer up, Brown Ears," said his loyal friend. "One day in your Uncle Ronald's chemist's shop won't be very hard work, and we can buy a feast of carrots with the money which he will pay us for our work!"

Brown Ears didn't look convinced.

"You never know, you might even enjoy it!" wheedled Grey Ears.

"Humph!" grunted Brown Ears.

"Oh well, I suppose you're right," said he in a grumpy voice. "I just hate to waste such a nice day, staying inside a mouldy old shop."

"Oh come on, Brown Ears!" scolded Grey Ears. "It's not a mouldy old shop. It's a very interesting place, full of wonderful pills and potions for curing every ailment, and remember, you'll look very handsome indeed in your nice white coat!"

Grey Ears knew just the right things to say to cheer Brown Ears up, and by the time they had reached Uncle Ronald's shop, ready for their day's work, Brown Ears was full of his usual high spirits and good humour. (He was also very keen to put on the white coat. He liked to think he was handsome!)

But what can this be? Our two work-shy rabbit friends about to do some honest toil?

Have they turned over a new leaf?

Have they mended their ways?

Is this going to mean an end to the tales of their mischief?

No!

Where Brown Ears and Grey Ears go, trouble usually follows, and this time was no exception.

There was trouble in store for the two rascals, sure enough.

Big trouble!

But they did not expect trouble when they arrived at the shop and greeted Uncle Ronald.   And nor did Uncle Ronald!

Brown Ears greeted his uncle warmly.

"Uncle Ronald, you can trust us completely," he reassured the old rabbit. "You look tired and pale. Go and have a peaceful day off work, sitting in the sunshine outside in your garden, and leave everything else to us."

Uncle Ronald looked just a little bit suspicious. He was very fond of Brown Ears but he knew very well that he was always up to mischief. Still, he was giving the rabbits a straightforward enough task. . . .

"Well, yes, Brown Ears, I shall have a nice day off, and thank you for your good wishes," he replied. "But I must give you some instructions before I go home. Listen carefully, for what I have to say is very important."

Brown Ears nodded, hopping from foot to foot impatiently. He was dying to put on that smart white coat!

"Both of you must be careful," continued Uncle Ronald, "to ask for the right money for all the things that you sell. Everything has a price written on it. Most important of all, you are allowed to sell headache pills, cough drops, soap, shampoo and toothpaste from the packets on the shelves, but if anybody comes to you with a note from the doctor asking for medicine to be made specially, you must ask them politely to go to the chemist in the next village. You are not chemists, and you are not allowed to make up medicines. That would be dangerous, and it is also against the law!"

Grey Ears felt his paws trembling. He had a funny feeling something was going to go wrong.

He had forgotten about the pharmacy at the back of Uncle Ronald's shop. He had forgotten about the lotions and potions and powders and creams, the mixing bowls, the spoons, the pestles and mortars. He had forgotten about the temptations that such a place could hold for a meddlesome rabbit like Brown Ears.

"Have no fear, Uncle Ronald! We will manage just fine!" exclaimed Brown Ears as he and Grey Ears waved goodbye to the old rabbit.

"Goodbye, boys !" Uncle Ronald called back cheerily. "I shall think of you both hard at work while I relax in my garden." Off he went, happily looking forward to a pleasant day of rest.

Grey Ears heaved a sigh of despair. He had a feeling now that everything was going to go horribly wrong. But he also felt that he was not going to be able to do anything about it!

Brown Ears rushed inside and struggled into his white coat as fast as he could.

"Isn't this great, Grey Ears? Don't I look important?"

"Well . . . ." said Grey Ears nervously. He knew from the gleam in Brown Ears' eye that trouble was coming.

Brown Ears went out of the shop door and looked eagerly up and down the street.

"I hope some customers come soon !" he said excitedly. "This is going to be fun!"

"Oh – oh !" said Grey Ears to himself. "Here we go again!"

The first few customers were easy.   Mr Hedgehog called in to buy some oil to make his spines shiny.   Mrs Mouse called in for some soap; it was bath day at her house and she had six children to scrub clean, so she needed quite a lot ! Mrs Mole needed some ointment for her sore eyes – she always got sore eyes on sunny days as moles only really like the dark, so Uncle Ronald kept a plentiful supply on the shelves.   It all seemed to be quite easy, but in between customers, Brown Ears would pop into the pharmacy where Uncle Ronald made up all the medicines, and Grey Ears didn't like the look of things at all. When Brown Ears was in this sort of mood, he just couldn't behave sensibly.   Grey Ears knew he was going to do something silly but he just couldn't quite work out what . . . .

To occupy his mind with other things, Grey Ears set about dusting the shelves and polishing the rows and rows of shiny glass bottles and jars.   As he worked, he tried practising the names of some of the contents.   Many of them were very long and difficult to pronounce, and would normally have kept his concentration for some while.   But try as he might, Grey Ears could not concentrate properly.   He was too worried about Brown Ears. . . .

A little while later, Mrs Badger came along the street with her
shopping basket.   She stopped at the door of the shop and came in.
   "I wonder if you can help me, young man," she said to Grey Ears.
"Mr Badger has been digging so much recently that his paws are all red
and raw.   Have you any cream to put on them to soothe them?"
Before Grey Ears could answer, Brown Ears pounced.   "I know of a
very secret formula to help just such a problem!" he announced.
"Come back in fifteen minutes and I shall have it ready for you!"

Grey Ears put his head between his paws and sighed. There was no
stopping Brown Ears!

Quick as a flash, Brown Ears was into the pharmacy, sloshing things
round in jars, squeezing things out of tubes, stirring, shaking, mixing,
making a glorious green gooey mess. He slopped it all into a little tub,
and when Mrs Badger came back, he gave it to her proudly, saying,
"Spread it on thickly, Mrs Badger, and it will make his paws as good as
new in no time!"

Grey Ears groaned in despair.

Things were quiet in the shop for the rest of the afternoon, and Grey Ears was just beginning to think that Brown Ears' foolishness would not be found out when a very angry Dr Squirrel came to the door of the shop, shaking his fist at the two rabbits in his fury.

"Which one of you made up that dreadful stuff to put on Mr Badger's paws.   Come on, own up immediately!"

Grey Ears could feel his heart thudding faster.

"It was—um—both of us!" said Brown Ears, crossing his paws behind his back.

"It was not, Brown Ears! It was you! I didn't even want to watch you doing it, it was such a silly thing to do!" protested Grey Ears.

"Oh well, I suppose it was me," admitted Brown Ears, shaking a little with fear now.

"Well, let me tell you, Brown Ears," cried Dr Squirrel, "that your 'ointment', as you had the nerve to call it, has made poor Mr Badger's paws come out in the most painful spots and blisters! He can hardly move his paws because they are so sore. You did a very wicked and dangerous thing, and we can only think ourselves lucky that you didn't make Mr Badger very ill indeed! I hope you realise how serious this is!"

"Oh yes I do, Dr Squirrel, and I am truly sorry. Please don't tell my uncle!" begged Brown Ears.

"I am afraid I had to call him in to make some more ointment up to soothe poor Mr Badger's sore paws. Look, here he comes now!"

Grey Ears cast a glance at Brown Ears. He could see now that his friend was swiftly beginning to regret his foolish actions. But it was too late for regrets now. The damage was done, and he was going to have to pay the price.

"Oh dear" whimpered Brown Ears. "Oh dear, oh dear, oh dear!"

They could see Uncle Ronald marching towards the shop door. And Constable Weasel was with him!

Uncle Ronald stormed into the shop, closely followed by Constable
Weasel.   By this time Brown Ears was shaking from head to toe.
Grey Ears just didn't know where to look.   Uncle Ronald was furious.
He announced that not only would the two rabbits get no pay for their
day's work, but that he was going to ask Constable Weasel to lock
Brown Ears in the village jail for a night to teach him a lesson.
Constable Weasel slunk away to get his handcuffs . . . .

"There, that's that !" said Constable Weasel once Brown Ears was
safely locked up for the night.   Quite a crowd was gathering round the
jail, curious to know what was going on.

"Let us just be thankful that Ronald Rabbit only left Brown Ears in
charge for one day!" quacked Mrs Duck.   The others nodded in
agreement.

That evening Brown Ears had a stream of visitors from the village, as he sat in his miserable, dark cell. Every one of them gave him a stern talking to about the error of his ways.

"I wish they would go away and leave me alone!" he muttered. "I need some sleep!"

"Perhaps this will teach you a lesson after all, Brown Ears," said Dr Squirrel.

Brown Ears' ears drooped.

254

Next morning, bright and early, Grey Ears appeared at Brown Ears' cell window.   He had not dared to visit his friend the night before in case he was locked up too! He thrust a crisp green lettuce through the window. "Here – breakfast!" he said cheerily, "How are you anyway?"

"I feel awful," said Brown Ears, "My head hurts and my bones ache !"

"Cheer up, Brown Ears," said his friend.   "You'll be let out soon, and when you get home you can make yourself some nice medicine!"

"That's *not* funny!" said Brown Ears, "*not funny at all* !"

Nanny Nonsense

Brown Ears was looking very glum indeed.   His tummy was rumbling with hunger.   He hadn't had anything to eat for a long time and, as so often happened, he and his little friend Grey Ears had no food in the store cupboard and no money in their pockets.

For the third time that day Grey Ears checked every nook and cranny in the kitchen in search of a morsel to eat, but to no avail.   All he could find were spiders' webs and a dusty, sticky old empty bottle that had once had some nettle cordial in it a very long time ago.

"It's no good, Brown Ears, we'll have to get a job somewhere to earn some money. We can't even go pilfering in the allotments because Harry Hedgehog has started keeping guard all day to stop us from stealing the vegetables. If we don't earn some money we'll starve!" Grey Ears was most distressed.

"I agree with you, Grey Ears, we do need a job. But who will employ us nowadays? After that disaster in Uncle Ronald's chemist shop, nobody will trust us!" Brown Ears went and looked gloomily out of the window at all the animals scurrying about in the streets below. They all seemed so busy and happy, doing their shopping, chatting or hurrying to their work. It all made Brown Ears feel even more depressed! Then, suddenly, he had an idea. His face lit up with delight. "What a clever little rabbit I am!" he thought to himself and turned back to where his little friend sat, miserable and hungry.

"No need for that gloomy face, Grey Ears!" he cried. "I have a solution to all our worries!"

Grey Ears looked a little doubtful. When Brown Ears looked like that, there was always trouble to follow! "What is the solution then, Brown Ears?" he asked hesitantly

"Well," said Brown Ears. "Do you remember that when we were in the Post Office yesterday we saw a notice that Mrs Fox had pinned up, asking for a nanny to help her to care for her four children?"

"Yes," replied Grey Ears. "But what has that got to do with us?"

"One of us can be the nanny!" exclaimed Brown Ears. "All we need are some of Rosie Rabbit's old clothes!"

And before Grey Ears had time to protest, Brown Ears was off like a shot, running all the way to Rosie Rabbit's house, leaving Grey Ears with his mouth wide open in surprise and disbelief. "He can't be serious!" thought Grey Ears. "He just can't be serious!"

But when Brown Ears returned with his arms full of old clothes from Rosie Rabbit, Grey Ears realised that he was quite serious. "I told Rosie I wanted them for a jumble sale," said Brown Ears. "Now, Grey Ears, you'll have to try them on."

"Me!" exclaimed Grey Ears. "You must be joking! I'm *not* going to put any frilly dress on. It's your idea, Brown Ears, *you* put it on!"

"Very well," said Brown Ears. "I shall!"

Grey Ears followed him up to the bedroom where Brown Ears struggled into one of Rosie Rabbit's dresses. It took him quite a long time to work out which way round it went on, and it took him even longer to fasten all the tiny buttons up the back.

Finally he went over to the mirror to take a look at himself. Grey Ears was trying very hard not to laugh.

Brown Ears looked very silly indeed!

"This is ridiculous!" cried Brown Ears. "These clothes are far too small for me! I'm sorry, Grey Ears, but you're going to have to be the nanny! Rosie Rabbit's clothes will fit you much better, and if we want to earn some money, you're going to have to do it!"

Brown Ears was secretly rather pleased!

With a lot of moaning and grumbling Grey Ears got himself dressed in the frilly dress and apron that Brown Ears had selected for him. Brown Ears was right. It did fit him much better.

"Right, Grey Ears!" said his friend. "Time to apply for your new job! Just remember to speak in a high voice to sound like a lady rabbit! Tell Mrs Fox that your name is. . . Rowena!" Brown Ears grinned. "You look very pretty, you know!"

Shortly afterwards, Grey Ears and Brown Ears arrived at Mrs Fox's house.   Brown Ears hid in the bushes while Grey Ears knocked on the door.   When Mrs Fox answered, she looked absolutely delighted.

"Have you come about the job?" she asked.   "Wonderful! These children are tiring me out – you can start right away!"   And she ushered Grey Ears into the house without even asking his name.

When they got inside, Grey Ears realised at once why Mrs Fox was so desperate for some help with her children. They were running wild all over the house.

"Children!" she screamed as she raced up the stairs to stop one of them from jumping off the landing. "This lady has come to look after you! Come and say hello!"

They all ran away and hid.

"I must go to the shops," announced Mrs Fox. "Take the children up to the nursery and play with them until I come back!" With that, she bustled off, leaving Grey Ears all alone with the four naughty fox cubs.

It took poor Grey Ears a long time to gather them all together and herd them into the nursery. He had never worked so hard in his life! Before long he was covered in sticky, fox-cub paw prints, and was bruised and battered from being jumped upon.

"Ow!" he shrieked as one of them bit his leg. "Can't we play a nice gentle game, children?" But the four little foxes just kept charging round, climbing on the furniture and fighting. "Calm down, children, please!" begged Grey Ears, trying to keep his voice as high and ladylike as possible.

It seemed like an age before Mrs Fox came back from the shops.
Grey Ears was just looking forward to a nice little rest, but Mrs Fox had
more work for him to do. "You can take the children to the park now!"
she said and bundled them all out of the front door.

"Try to tire them out as much as possible, and don't come back
before teatime!"

Poor Grey Ears! His head was aching from all the noise and
commotion!

How Grey Ears survived until the end of the day, he did not know, but at last the fox cubs were all fed and bathed and tucked up in bed fast asleep.   Mrs Fox decided to take the opportunity to leave Grey Ears to babysit while she went out for a stroll with Mr Fox, who had arrived home from work at teatime.   Grey Ears helped himself to a tasty snack from the kitchen, and then settled himself cosily in front of the fire.

"Hey there, Grey Ears!" came a shout from the window. It was Brown Ears.

"Seems like you've got an easy job there!" he said.

"Not at all, I'll have you know that I have been working very hard indeed!" protested Grey Ears, and he showed Brown Ears the bruises and bites and scratches he had received that afternoon from the fox cubs.

"Never mind all that!" scoffed Brown Ears. "At least you've had something to eat! Now off you go and get something from the kitchen for me!"

Grey Ears got up and went through to the kitchen as he had been asked.

"Do you want some poppy seed cake, Brown Ears?" he called through to his friend. Unthinking, he forgot to use his high-pitched ladylike voice, and at that very moment Mrs Fox appeared through the back door, home from her walk with her husband. She heard Grey Ears calling to his friend. For the first time that day she took a proper look at her "nanny" and recognised Grey Ears in disguise. She was furious!

"Rowena, eh? We'll see about that!" She marched Grey Ears down to the cellar. "You can just spend the night down here, and first thing in the morning Mr Fox will take you to the police station and Constable Weasel will sort out your punishment. You are an imposter!" she shouted.

"Do you think you could give me my pay for my work before you shut me in for the night?" asked Grey Ears nervously, hopefully holding out an empty envelope.

"*Certainly not!*" yelled Mrs Fox, and she slammed the cellar door shut, locking it tight before she stormed back upstairs.

"Brown Ears, Brown Ears, where are you?" called Grey Ears.

Brown Ears, who had been hiding in the bushes to avoid all the commotion, appeared at the window.

"Get me out of here, *please*, Brown Ears!" begged Grey Ears.
"She's locked me in, and she's going to take me to Constable Weasel
in the morning! I've got to escape."

"Have no fear, little friend, I'll think of something!" Brown Ears assured him. "You stay there and don't worry, I'll get you out, I promise!" Brown Ears' head disappeared from sight, and Grey Ears could hear the gentle thump of his friend's paws as he slipped off into the night.

Grey Ears sat down miserably among the piles of clutter stored in Mr and Mrs Foxs' cellar.

"Oh yes, Brown Ears, I'll stay here. I *have* to stay here. I can't go

anywhere, because I can't get out!" he muttered gloomily to himself.

He was cross with himself for listening to Brown Ears' plan to pretend to be a nanny.   Yet again, Brown Ears had got him into trouble.

"If Brown Ears doesn't get me out of here soon, I shall never speak to him again!" he declared out loud.

"If Brown Ears doesn't get me out of here soon, I shall be in *big* trouble!" he thought to himself miserably.

Brown Ears, meanwhile, was hurrying home as fast as his little legs would carry him. He had an idea that just might help his little friend to escape. He was feeling rather guilty, for he knew that it was his fault that Grey Ears was in trouble, and he knew that if Grey Ears didn't escape before morning, more trouble would follow when Constable Weasel found out what had been going on!

If Constable Weasel became involved then he would be sure to guess that Grey Ears had not got up to this little exploit on his own. And who would he come looking for? Brown Ears, of course!

He hurried into the house, collected what he needed, and headed back to Mrs Fox's house at top speed.

Shortly afterwards, Brown Ears arrived at the Foxs' house, carrying Grey Ears' clothes and a little bell in his paws. He hid himself in the bushes a little way from the house, and began ringing the bell.

"Come and see the magic show!" he called. "Watch the rabbit disappear! Come and see the magic show!" He carried on ringing and calling out until Mr and Mrs Fox came to the door to see what all the noise was about.

"What's going on?" Mr Fox asked his wife.

Brown Ears kept on ringing the bell. "Magic show! Watch the rabbit disappear!" he called again.

"It sounds like the noise is coming from over there," said Mrs Fox, pointing to the bushes. "Let's take a look."

Slowly the two foxes came towards where Brown Ears was hiding. Brown Ears rang the bell one more time. "Watch the rabbit disappear!" he called, and grabbing Grey Ears' clothes, he ducked round the side of the bushes, sneaked behind Mr and Mrs Fox and dived down to their cellar. Quick as a flash he unlocked the cellar door, grabbed Grey Ears, and hauled him out of the house and off towards the woods.

"The rabbit has *disappeared*!" he called out as they ran off. The two puzzled foxes were still searching round the bushes!

The two rabbits headed for the safety and darkness of the woods, where Mr and Mrs Fox would not be able to find them. Brown Ears, after all the running about that he had been doing, was by this time very breathless and hot, but even in his discomfort he took pleasure from the clever trick that he had played on Mr and Mrs Fox to help Grey Ears escape.

"Disappearing rabbit – ha, ha!" he chortled as he ran.

Once they were well into the woods, Grey Ears changed back into his own clothes, and the rascally pair of rabbits sped home.

Once they were safely back at their own house, Grey Ears turned crossly to Brown Ears.

"I suppose I should thank you for rescuing me, but don't you *ever* make me do anything like that *ever* again!"

Brown Ears looked a little sheepish. "I'm sorry, Grey Ears, truly I am, but at least you got a decent meal before you were found out! I'm still hungry!"

"T*oo bad!*" said Grey Ears, and the two rabbits went inside to bed.

The Poet

It was a beautiful sunny day, and Grey Ears had just spent a very busy morning in his cousin Rosie Rabbit's garden, hoeing the vegetable patch.   In return for all his hard work, Rosie had given the little rabbit a whole bagful of carrots and courgettes and other delicious vegetables to take home and share with his friend.   Grey Ears was very pleased as he came whistling through the garden gate, but he suddenly stopped in surprise as a very strange sight met his eyes.   There was Brown Ears, sitting at the garden table with a towel wrapped round his head! There were sheets of paper all around him, and he was writing things down fast and furiously.   He seemed to be enjoying himself greatly.

"What on earth are you doing, Brown Ears?" asked Grey Ears.

"Ssh, Grey Ears! Please be quiet! Can't you see I'm concentrating?" said Brown Ears crossly.

"But why have you got a towel wrapped round your head?" Grey Ears couldn't keep quiet!

"It is *not* a towel, stupid! It's a *turban*!" said Brown Ears even more crossly. "When I wear it, I feel inspired to write great and magnificent things. But I can't write anything if you keep interrupting me like this!"

"Well, Brown Ears, I hope you won't mind one more interruption of your great work," said Grey Ears huffily, "for I have to tell you that while you have been playing around scribbling on bits of paper, I have done an honest morning's work in Rosie Rabbit's garden. I have earned us enough vegetables to make us a feast for lunch, but of course I suppose you may be too busy to eat anything. . ."

"All right, all right," said Brown Ears grudgingly. "Go and make my lunch! I need fuel for my brain after all. But I am *not* playing around! I am *working*!" And with that, he turned his attention once more to the paper in front of him.

"He's gone quite mad!" thought Grey Ears as he went into the kitchen to prepare the vegetables. "Quite, quite mad! Perhaps it's something he has eaten. Or perhaps he's ill – an infection of the brain? Should I call Dr Squirrel, I wonder? On the other hand, it's much more likely that he's off on another of his crazy schemes. I shall need a good lunch if I'm going to have to put up with him behaving like that all day!"

He looked out of the window at Brown Ears scribbling away in the garden.   "And he looks very, very silly with that turban round his head!" Grey Ears smiled to himself.   Life was certainly never dull with Brown Ears around!   But what was his "work" supposed to be?   What "great and magnificent thing" was Brown Ears supposed to be writing?

Grey Ears could contain his curiosity no longer. He tiptoed out into the garden and sneaked a look over Brown Ear's shoulder. It was really hard to read Brown Ear's writing, because it was very untidy and scrawly, but Grey Ears could make out from the groups of lines that Brown Ears had already written that his friend was writing a poem of some sort. "Poetry!" shrieked Grey Ears. "You're writing poetry!"

Brown Ears, who had been too busy to notice Grey Ears creeping up on him, practically jumped out of his fluffy brown rabbit skin!

"Oh! Ah! Grey Ears, you startled me. You shouldn't creep up on me like that. And you shouldn't be so nosey!"

"Aw, come on, Brown Ears," Grey Ears coaxed his friend. "Show me some of your work, please! Let me read it!"

"Well. . . ." Brown Ears hesitated. He was secretly delighted that Grey Ears wanted to see his work, but he didn't want to appear over-eager.

"Allright," he said at last. "You may read one poem – or, better still, I shall read it to you!" Solemnly Brown Ears cleared his throat and began:

"What a friendly place our village is,
How nice it is to live here.
We all are honest creatures
And always full of fun and happiness."

281

He stopped reading and looked at Grey Ears expectantly. "Well, what do you think?" he demanded.

Grey Ears looked at his feet and thought for a moment. He did not want to hurt Brown Ears' feelings, but he could hardly pretend that the poem was the magnificent work that Brown Ears thought it was.

"Oh – um – quite nice, Brown Ears!" he finally said. "Perhaps it needs a little more work on it – you know – to make it rhyme or something?"

Brown Ears looked indignant for a moment, and then nodded slowly.

"Yes, I see what you mean, Grey Ears. It is only a first try, of course. I shall be looking at my work again and again as I go along, to rewrite some parts, to change a word here or there, and to help me choose the best of my poems."

"What for?" asked Grey Ears.

"For the talent competition at the town gala, of course!" exclaimed Brown Ears.

Grey Ears smiled. He had forgotten all about the competition. Every year at the town gala several of the animals in the town would perform for the rest of Whiskerton, and whichever act was judged best by the Mayor would win a lovely prize.

Brown Ears had always longed to win the talent competition. Last year he had tried a juggling act with carrots but had dropped every

single carrot.   The year before that he had tried acrobatics but had fallen from a handstand and had been left with a swollen nose and two black eyes for a week.   The year before that, he had tried to do a magic show but his "magical exploding wand" had singed his eyebrows.   Now, this year, it was to be poetry!   Well, Grey Ears thought to himself, Brown Ears didn't give up easily!

"At least you can't hurt yourself reading poems!" Grey Ears grinned.

"I am going to *win* reading poems!" announced his chum, and sat down with pen and paper once more.

"Well, well, well," thought Grey Ears to himself.   "I wonder if he will win?"

Days passed, and Brown Ears' excitement grew greater with every passing minute.   All day long he sat at his table, scribbling, scrawling, sometimes scrubbing out.   Occasionally he would stop and think, and then with a cry of "That's it!" or "Of course!", or "I've got it!", he would start scribbling again.

And all the time, day and night, he kept the towel wrapped round his head.

"What's Brown Ears up to now?" Harry Hedgehog asked Grey Ears one day.

"Oh, it's his idea for trying to win the talent competition," giggled Grey Ears. "He's trying to write poetry!"

"I am writing poetry!" interrupted Brown Ears. "And it's getting better all the time! Listen to this. . . ."

"Twinkle, twinkle, Henry Hare
Isn't here, he's over there,
But when he's somewhere else, I fear,
He can be neither there nor here.

I'm particularly proud of that poem!"

"Very funny, Brown Ears, very funny!" said Harry Hedgehog.

"It isn't meant to be funny!" shrieked Brown Ears.   "It's a serious poem!   It is quite clear to me that you, Harry Hedgehog, and all other creatures like you, have simply no taste when it comes to the fine things in life.   You wouldn't know a good poem if you came across it in your soup!"

"I should indeed be furious if I came across a poem in my soup!" retorted Harry Hedgehog. "I like vegetables in my soup, not soggy bits of paper!"

Grey Ears smothered a giggle and quickly bustled Harry Hedgehog away before he and Brown Ears began to fight.

"Mad, mad, absolutely mad!" muttered Harry Hedgehog.

As they left they could hear Brown Ears talking to himself.

"Soup! Great idea! Let's see now. . . .

There's nothing like a bowl of soup
Fills you up and makes you p. . .
-No, no, can't have that. . ."

Grey Ears laughed out loud.

285

The next day Dr. Squirrel called round.

"Ah! Dr Squirrel!" cried Brown Ears. "I've just been writing about you! Listen to this. . .

> Doctor, Doctor send a letter
> To the chemist
> Make me better!"

Grey Ears rolled his eyes in disbelief.

Dr Squirrel looked over the top of his spectacles at Brown Ears.

(He always looked this way when considering something serious.)

"Brown Ears," he declared finally after a pause, "you have definitely been overdoing things. I think you should stop all this – um –" (he waved his hand towards the piles of paper surrounding Brown Ears) "All this – um – ah – writing stuff. It's making you behave rather strangely!"

Brown Ears snorted loudly. "Pah! You don't mean that at all, Dr Squirrel! I happen to know for a fact that your dear nephew Sammy is entering the contest with his display of card tricks. You are merely concerned that if I enter Sammy won't have a chance of winning!"

Dr Squirrel shrugged his shoulders. "I can see that there is no point in talking to him when he's like this," he said to Grey Ears. "But please do treat him gently. I worry that if this goes on much longer he will go completely batty!"

"Don't worry, Doctor" said Grey Ears, grinning. "Brown Ears gets like this from time to time when he sees a way of getting a free feast. The mood will pass – it always does!"

"What exactly do you mean – when he sees a way of getting a free feast?" asked Dr Squirrel, puzzled.

"Oh, haven't you heard?" said Grey Ears "The prize this year for the best entry in the talent competition is a banquet for two cooked by Mrs Mole!"

"Mm – delicious. . ." mumbled Dr Squirrel, and he wandered away, shaking his head in amazement.

Brown Ears went on scribbling and muttering.

Grey Ears turned to go inside and make some tea, then paused for a moment, deep in thought. A feast at Mrs Mole's. . . truly wonderful! He could just imagine it – crisp, multicoloured salads, sumptuous stews, scalding-hot soups, gooey puddings, dandelion wine, all bubbly and delicious. . . . He shook himself out of his reverie.

Of course, Grey Ears himself did not believe for a moment that Brown Ears had a chance of winning, but there was always a slight possibility of a miracle happening!

News did not take long to get around about Brown Ears' doings. Before long he had become known as "The Mad Poet", and the other animals would point and giggle as he strutted along the street with his ridiculous headgear on. As he went he was continually muttering away to himself as he tried to think of more and more, better and better poems.

> "Oh rabbits love lettuce
> Dum-de-dum-de-dum....
> We'd eat yours if you'd let us
> De-dum-de-doo-di-dum..."

Needless to say, his poems did not get better and better. They were all really rather dreadful, but Brown Ears just did not seem to realise this. He carried on regardless, practising and practising for the great day when he intended to take the talent contest by storm with what he thought was his astounding talent. He was so sure that he was going to win, so utterly convinced that the first prize was his for the taking, that he could almost taste the mouth-watering dishes that he imagined himself tucking into at Mrs Mole's after the contest.

The night before the contest, the rabbit household was buzzing with activity. Mind you, there was only one rabbit that was causing all the fuss – Grey Ears could do nothing but sit and watch in amazement as Brown Ears rushed hither and thither, sifting through the piles and piles of paper that littered the floors of their little house. Now and then he would crumple up a piece of paper and hurl it at the wastepaper basket, at other times he would come across a poem which he thought was particularly good, give a cry of "This is a winner!" and put it in a corner of the room along with the others that he wanted to read in the competition. Then he would change his mind, throw another poem here, save another poem there.

Finally, after what seemed like hours of rustling and crumpling and shuffling, Brown Ears was left with three piles of paper on the floor. One pile was an enormous heap of crumpled bits, (the wastepaper basket was somewhere underneath it); another was a pile of poems that he intended to read at the talent contest; the last pile was "for emergencies."

"What does "for emergencies" mean ?" Grey Ears asked.

"You never know, Grey Ears," the "Mad Poet" insisted, "I may be required to give an encore after the contest, so I must have some spare poems ready to read!"

Grey Ears suddenly felt that he couldn't take any more, and he disappeared off to bed, but Brown Ears still had some preparation to do for the big day.

For two whole weeks, Brown Ears had worn his towel around his head like a turban, day and night, without taking it off. Now, he finally removed it. He gave it a good wash and hung it out to dry. Then he gave his head a good scrub and brushed his long brown ears until they shone. When he was finally satisfied that all was well and ready for the morning, he went to his bed and dreamed of vegetable soup and rhubarb tarts.

On the morning of the contest Brown Ears was up at the crack of dawn, his turban, now clean, back on his head and his poems checked and rechecked.   After breakfast, he stuck his head out of his bedroom window to see the world going by.   Constable Weasel was passing.

"Morning, Constable! Coming to see me win the talent contest today, are you?" he called cheekily.

"I hardly think you will win reading a few dreary old poems!" scoffed Constable Weasel.

"Maybe so, Constable Weasel, but like Mrs Mole's cooking, my poems have a secret something special about them!" he retorted airily.

"Come on, Grey Ears," he called to his friend. "Let's call on Mrs Mole on our way to the gala!"

"Are you sure this is a good idea, coming to see what I am preparing for the winner's feast?" asked Mrs Mole when the two rabbits arrived. "You might not win after all, Brown Ears!"

"With its secret something special, my poetry *must* win!" exclaimed Brown Ears.

"Secret something special – what's that?" asked Grey Ears, sniffing at a wonderful-smelling pot of soup on the stove.

"You'll see," beamed Brown Ears. "You'll see!"

291

The gala was a very festive occasion indeed. There were stalls with home baking, flowers and handcrafts. There were acrobats and jugglers. There were competitions of all sorts. Grey Ears walked around everything with his friend, taking in the atmosphere of revelry, enjoying the fun of it all. Brown Ears, on the other hand, was too excited to pay attention to anything much. He was all of a twitter, waiting for his great moment.

Finally, it was time for the talent competition. Everybody gathered round to watch, and in a special seat, marked RESERVED, sat the Mayor of Whiskerton, Sir Wallace Weasel. He was going to judge the contest.

It was all most entertaining, really, thought Grey Ears to himself. Harry Hedgehog was first, playing a tune with his bristles on some jam jars filled up to different levels with water. Then came Mrs Mouse, tap dancing on a tiny wooden platform which her husband had specially built for her. Constable Weasel surprised everyone by coming up on stage and telling a few jokes, but they weren't very funny, to tell the truth. Mr Badger put on quite a good Punch and Judy show. Sammy Squirrel's card tricks were absolutely wonderful and had everybody gasping with admiration.

Grey Ears saw the Mayor clapping enthusiastically, and decided to forget the feast at Mrs Mole's. Brown Ears could not possibly win, he had decided.

Finally, it was Brown Ears' turn to perform. Instead of simply going on stage like the other animals had done, Brown Ears got up and walked to the Punch and Judy booth which had been put to one side after Mr Badger's performance. He clambered in and stuck his head and shoulders out of the top! He looked very strange indeed, and Grey Ears heard the Mayor give a little cough to try to hide his giggles. Brown Ears didn't notice.

"Ladies and gentlemen," he announced. "As you all know, I have spent a great deal of time composing some poetry to read to you all today. Some of you may think that poems are boring to listen to – even if they are as brilliant as mine! Therefore, I have decided to make my poems come alive for you today, by putting them to music. I am going to sing to you my 'Musical Odes to Whiskerton'."

"*Oh no!*" thought Grey Ears. "*Oh no!*" You see, Grey Ears knew that Brown Ears couldn't sing a note in tune. Brown Ears' singing was absolutely dreadful! "He can't be *serious!*" thought Grey Ears. But he was!

With a pause to clear his throat Brown Ears began;

"Ow–ow– ow–oh–I am a lucky rabb–eeet!"

he bellowed.

"Ay–ee–ay– ee–ay live in Whiss–ss–sskerton!"

he yelled.

"You–oo–oo won't find me–hee at hoho–home today–ee!"

he screeched.

"Can yoohoo guess wha–ha–here I've gone?"

he brayed.

Grey Ears covered his ears and shut his eyes tight.

Brown Ears carried on;

"Thees fair tow–oon has a g–halah!

A talent ca–hontest too–hoo!"

he whinnied.

"So come and liss–ss–sten careflee–ee!

Yoo - hoo'll hear what ay - ee can doo–hoo!"

Oh, the shame of it! How was Grey Ears going to live it down? Brown Ears had embarrassed him before, but never as badly as this! Oh, the shame!

Now, even with his ears covered, sounds of Brown Ears' terrible singing were getting through to Grey Ears, and then suddenly he realised that over the singing he could just make out another sound, the sound of laughter. He opened his eyes and took his paws away from his ears. He had expected to hear boos and jeers, but not laughter! He looked around and saw everyone, including the Mayor, clutching their sides and shaking with laughter. Too carried away with himself to notice this, Brown Ears bawled and shouted and warbled on from poem to poem. When finally he finished, he was quite breathless, but flushed with triumph at his great moment.

The audience, helpless with laughter, could hardly find the strength to clap.

At last, the Mayor took control.

"Ladies and gentlemen, I have finished my judging!" he announced.

"I have decided to award not one, but *two* prizes!" Everyone listened.

"First prize for skill and talent must go, I feel, to Sammy Squirrel! Ladies and gentlemen, Sammy Squirrel!"

Everyone clapped as Sammy went up to shake the Mayor's hand. Brown Ears began to splutter with indignation, but Grey Ears glared at him to keep quiet.

"The next prize must, I feel, also be a special prize, to the performer who gave me the best laugh I have had in years. I shall tell Mrs. Mole to prepare a special banquet for him and his friend. Ladies and gentlemen – Brown Ears!" The audience cheered.

"Laugh?" whispered Brown Ears to his friend. "Did they really *laugh*? - At my poetry? – At my singing?"

"Never mind, Brown Ears!" whispered his friend. "Don't you see, it doesn't matter one bit if they laughed? You've won a special prize! A banquet at Mrs Mole's!"

"I have, have I? Oh well. . . ."

"*Take it*!" Grey Ears nudged him. "Go and shake the Mayor's hand before he changes his mind! Quickly!"

And with that, Grey Ears grabbed the pile of papers from his friend's paws and shoved him over towards the Mayor to be congratulated.

The miracle had happened. Brown Ears had won (well sort of!). Grey Ears was delighted.

That night, at Mrs Mole's banquet, Brown Ears had recovered a little. He had got over the fact that nobody took his poetry seriously – well, nearly got over it. But he thought he might just have one more recital before he tucked into the feast.

"Oh, Mrs Mole, oh cooky–doo. . ." he began.

"Oh do be *quiet* and sit down at the table, or all this lovely food will be spoiled!" interrupted Grey Ears.

And that was the last anyone heard of Brown Ears' poetry.
Thank goodness!